THE GIRL FROM WONDERLAND

C.G. LAMBERT

Copyright © 2021 by C.G. Lambert

First paperback edition September 2021

Published by Clamp Ltd

Set in Junicode and Trade Gothic

Cover Art by Nick Castle

ISBN 978-1-914531-20-0 Paperback (IngramSpark)

ISBN 978-1-914531-21-7 Hardback

ISBN 978-1-914531-20-0 Paperback (Amazon)

ISBN 978-1-914531-23-1 ePUB

www.cglambert.com

www.clamp.pub

For Matt, Todd, Bryan & Duds

CONTENTS

ACKNOWLEDGMENTS

Even self-published novels have many people helping—and while every mistake is my own, the following people have been most helpful with their contributions:

Thanks to my beta readers—Andrew Grenfell & Parth Munjani for their insights and feedback.

Special thanks to my Sensitivity reader, Nicola Soremekun and my Police Advisors Robert Constable and my two friends from the Met. Expert advice is worth its weight in gold.

Thanks again to my Editor, Michael Thorn for his gentle guidance and advice.

Thanks again to Nick Castle for the great cover.

And always, thanks to my First Reader.

PROLOGUE

The kid went flying. Alice wasn't huge but she'd been sprinting at full pace and the kid had just walked out in front of her, giving her no chance to avoid him. She wanted to stop—to apologise, to make amends—but the impending catastrophe had to be stopped and so she sprinted off again, ignoring the shouts of abuse.

Far behind, Boris was yelling something as he sought to keep up, but Alice concentrated on trying to find the openings and gaps in the crowds. Regent Street was just stirring to life on another glorious summer morning and, while the pavements were nowhere near full, they still created a substantial obstacle to Alice's pursuit.

Lungs burning, Alice switched to running along the roadside. Finding fewer pedestrians but more bike couriers and buses pulling up at bus stops to disgorge passengers, she really didn't know if it was a better option than dodging shoppers on the pavement. Eventually, she decided they were both bad options and figured the narrow streets of Soho might be less congested. She left Regent Street but immediately regretted it. While there *was* less traffic, the pavements were narrower and the cars proportionally larger, meaning less space to make progress. And less room to weave in and out of pedestrians too. Grimacing, she found herself impatiently hopping from one foot to another as a suited office worker temporarily blocked her in a tunnel of scaffolding before she was able to break back into a sprint and almost collided with a taxi coming the other way.

Brushing past the side of the cab to the bemusement of the passenger and annoyance of the driver, she turned down into Carnaby Street, realising she didn't know which end of the pedestrian thoroughfare the delivery would be made. She caught her breath while checking her phone for the map of the delivery vehicle, praying that her headlong dash from the tube station had paid dividends.

Wiping sleep from her eyes, she zoomed in on the map and found the delivery vehicle already turning into Great Marlborough Street, at the other end of Carnaby Street! The map confirmed that was where the delivery would be made.

The sleepless night and lack of breakfast were starting to catch up with her, but she dug deep and steeled herself for the final push. She was able to make good progress along the pedestrian-only Carnaby Street and was just congratulating herself on a good choice of route when she saw the delivery van pull up ahead of her.

Yelling and waving to attract the driver's attention, she tried to ignore the early morning shoppers and office workers on their way to work carrying overly caffeinated Starbucks with misspelt names and realised she had no idea what to do next.

"Stop!" she managed as the driver got out and ignored her, heading to the back of the van. "Really, you have to stop!" she insisted, but the guy—dressed in the delivery company's livery and with one earbud dangling from an ear—kept moving, grabbing the handle for the roller door at the rear of the truck.

"Hey!" she yelled, getting uncomfortably close to the driver's face, so much so that he finally registered her presence and blinked in surprise. "You cannot open that door. It's a matter of life and death. Do *not* open that door."

Finally gathering himself, the driver held up his clipboard. "Fuck off lady, I've got a delivery to make."

"No, really," she persisted, "if you open that door, everybody on this street will die."

He hesitated, obviously weighing up in his mind whether she was a nutcase or if there was even a sliver of a chance of there being an actual danger. Decision made, he wrenched the roller door up and continued, exposing the interior full of brown cardboard boxes and parcels.

"If you don't leave, I'll have to call the cops," he said matter-of-factly, grabbing one of the handles on the rear of the truck ready to vault up into the cavernous cargo compartment.

The puffing behind her manifested itself into Boris. Hands on his knees, he wheezed his anger at her. "What the fuck were you going to do? What if the cars had come out of the packages?" he managed between breaths.

Alice was lost. They'd identified the threat and she was trying to neutralise it, but then she realised how little she could do. If the parcels had hatched, spawning their deadly cargo, she would have been nothing more than the first in a long list of casualties. The fact that she had got to them before they'd been delivered was only a saving grace if she could persuade the driver not to deliver—and, of course, she had no authority. She was just some nutcase ranting about death with no badge, no authority, nothing but a story delivered breathlessly with the conviction of a religious zealot or the truly insane.

Boris was talking to the delivery driver when the sirens in the distance came closer and police cars and vans hove into view, surrounding the delivery vehicle and erupting with uniformed police officers. They leapt into action, setting up yellow tape and shepherding the public away. One of them tried to move Alice along until Boris stepped in and beckoned for her to join him.

"Go home and get some sleep. You've done really well. It looks like we've stopped them in time. The other shipments have been isolated and we got the Stingray working so the cars couldn't connect."

Alice nodded slowly, standing in shock, swaying slightly. The adrenaline rush was subsiding, leaving her drained, empty. She'd had no food since the Chinese takeaway the previous night. The events of the last week were just starting to hit her.

JOB

Alice needed a job.

The weather in London was conspiring against her though. Since her return from Australia ten days ago, there'd been an unseasonal heatwave which was forecast to continue for the rest of the week. It had been a strong distraction from the job search, so Alice was now making a concerted effort. In addition to applying for more and more jobs online, she was also reconnecting with her network—which was how she found herself walking towards Clerkenwell for some after-work drinks with former work colleagues.

Alice was slightly above average height with long mousy hair. A lucky genetic makeup and careful diet kept her super slim. She wore large round glasses which gave her an owlish look and, while she normally wore a favourite checked long-sleeved shirt, the heat had made keeping it on unbearable, so she had wrapped it around her waist, revealing a generic tech company's T-shirt she'd got from their stand at one of a dozen trade shows she'd visited, its jokey slogan now faded beyond reading.

Alice had grown up in a town on the outskirts of London, far enough away to have its own identity, but close enough to be commutable for university. She shuddered to remember the ninety-minute trips each way— longer if you just missed the connection to the bus at the end of the underground on the way home. She'd started helping some of the clubs and societies at university with their web presence, building on skills she'd picked up at the local college, and had managed to parlay that into a series of contracting gigs which had helped pay her tuition fees. She could have lived on campus but had enjoyed spending time with her family. She'd been brought up by semi-retired parents. Dad had previously worked in a newspaper but now pottered in the garden or the shed, while Mum had been a teacher who still did some supply teaching here and there. They'd had Alice quite late in life which had made for them being misidentified as her grandparents all through her schooling— which was ironic, as she never had any relationship with her actual grandparents. Not long after graduation, her Mum had become bedridden with a persistent cold which turned into pneumonia which she had not been strong enough to fight off. She'd passed away and Dad hadn't lasted long after that so, two years ago, Alice had found herself an orphan with a degree, a small pot of money which had been left after selling the house and paying off the mortgage, and no idea on what to do next. Despite friends telling her to go travelling for a while, she really couldn't see the point, and so had emigrated to Australia driven by the assurance that it was 'practically England but with better weather'. That hadn't really worked out too well for her, so she found herself back in London during an unseasonal heatwave looking for work.

The afternoon sun had brought out all manner of office workers to the pubs tucked into every nook and cranny of London's historic streets. Workers, who would normally head straight to the train station for the hour-long journey back home to their houses in commuter towns, instead joined colleagues at the local for a quick cheeky pint.

As the pavements widened after the railway bridge, they were taken over by the British version of al-fresco drinking. Whereas on the continent suave roadside tables would allow debonair patrons to eat and drink while breathing in the fumes at exhaust pipe level, in the UK a few waist-height barriers created a corral of sorts, expanding the area where patrons were allowed to drink. Such was the communal delight at the heat, all of those areas were overrun and drinkers were perched wherever they could find a hard surface to lean on.

Alice was picking her way past one such cluster when she heard someone shriek her name.

"Alice!! Oh, it is you, I thought so! How long have you been back?!"

Alice zoomed in on the source, a tall brunette with a pixie-cut hairstyle and wearing a summer wrap dress. Alice had known Danica for ten years. While in high school, she'd been overweight but about five years ago she'd started going to the gym religiously and eating well. Now she was stunning. Alice had once asked her how she had done it and Danica had told her that whenever she looked at a candy bar and read that it had 100 calories, she didn't see that as an empty data point, or focus on the delicious five minutes that it would take to eat, but rather on the pain that an hour on the treadmill to burn it off would be like. When she saw food in terms of the amount of pain they represented, steering clear of the bad foods became very easy.

The group Danica was with were obviously workmates, some less discreetly checking her out than others. Glancing behind her, Danica grabbed Alice's arm and moved away from the noise of the pub's drinking area.

"Oh my god, it's good to see you! You'll have to tell me all about Oz. How was it? Are you just visiting or are you back for good?"

Alice waited for the stream of questions to, if not die out, then at least pause.

"I'm good actually, just got back. Looking for work, so meeting some friends for a drink."

Danica continued, "Oh my god, you won't believe what I've had to put up with! Some guy I was dating keeps sending me dick pics and I've had enough! I'm going to the police station tomorrow to make a complaint. You should come too!"

Alice started to reply that, while grateful for the offer, she couldn't think of a worse use of her time than waiting for someone else to make a complaint at a police station about pictures of penises when Danica pressed her case.

"Oh, you've got to come, you can tell me all about Oz and all that. And! And! I'm meeting with the Head of Programming at that travel company in

Soho for a coffee afterwards! So, you can come and meet her with me. Maybe she's got a job for you?!"

Alice took a second. Danica had a heart of gold, so while it took a lot of energy following her barrage of words and their abrupt change in topics, she was always good for a laugh. Plus, that travel company in Soho was high on the list of companies Alice had always wanted to work for. "Sure! Text me the address and time and I'll be there! It'll be great to catch up!"

"Cool! Are you on the same number?"

"Yep, same sim card, same number."

They hugged goodbye and Danica returned to the gated area with her beer.

Alice crossed the road at the pedestrian crossing and headed down a side street. Leather Lane usually had street stalls for the office lunch hour, but the lunch rush finished at 2pm, so the only remnants were a few cardboard boxes and swollen rubbish bags, awaiting collection. The pubs along the lane were like those on Clerkenwell Road—rammed.

Where she was going was on a side street off the side street. An elbow of a road connecting to Clerkenwell, used infrequently by cycle couriers and the odd lost taxi driver, it didn't need a gated section, the numbers of drinkers there being significantly fewer than on the main drag. Come to think of it, every time she'd been to the Hat and Tun, the number of drinkers never seemed to change.

Standing outside the pub, drinks-in-hand, were three people she knew and one she did not. They were all of a similar age—in their early thirties, she would guess.

Jeremy was tall and slim, with the gaunt look of a long-distance runner. He was the head of the design team at the bank where they'd met. Alice grinned as she remembered the pressure he'd been under to release the app they'd been working on, and how Jeremy had held out because he wanted to make it accessible—so that screen readers could interact with it for the blind, and so that the colour combinations worked for the colour-blind, that sort of thing. After resisting senior management pressure for months, ignoring subtle threats to career, life, and limb, they'd finally released the app. Then six months later the awards started to come in. The senior managers preened and basked in the glory of the awards while the design team shook their heads at the undeserved accolades.

The other two she knew were of average height and also of slim build. Tang and Roy headed up the contract design team which had done the work on the app back then. They were seldom seen apart and so had taken on the portmanteau of "Troy". Commonly heard questions back then had been, "Have you seen Troy? What did Troy say?" While Roy matched the casual dress code favoured by Jeremy, Tang was in typical designer gear of a black polo neck—and looked like he was feeling the effects of the heatwave because of it.

As for the last guy, she hadn't seen him before. He was tall like Jeremy but had a burgeoning potbelly suggesting a career sitting at a desk. He too was in casual gear (T-shirt and jeans)—the shirt emblazoned with the logo of a tech firm long since gone out of business. Alice suspected that he thought this was supposed to afford him some sort of geek street cred before she realised the same could be said of herself.

Greeting them each in turn, Alice waited to be introduced to the new guy.

"Barry, this is Alice, she's just returned from Australia and she's a coder."

"And what do you do, Barry?" Alice inquired politely.

He looked surprised at the question for some reason. "I don't quite know how to describe it."

Alice frowned. "You don't know what you do?" she asked.

"I just don't know the right way of answering," he said, looking over to Jeremy.

"I used to say, 'I make things better'," suggested Jeremy.

"Heh," said Dan, "I used to say I'm a hippo killer."

"Wha?" riposted Barry. "A hippo killer?"

"Yeah - HiPPO: Highest Paid Person's Opinion."

Barry looked confused. So, Tang continued.

"Look: at the highest levels you get feedback from clients who have no idea of design principles or what makes good design. Everyone has an opinion, obviously. And so everybody defers to their boss, hence the opinion which matters most belongs to the Highest Paid Person in the room. And if you let those people make decisions, you will end up with something which you really don't want to put your name on."

"So how do you kill the HiPPO?" Barry frowned.

"Research. You say 'Sure we could add a marquee tag there and have the text bounce around the screen. But *this* research says that's a bad idea and *this* says it has a detrimental effect on customer experience'. You depersonalise it. And you establish that you know what you're talking about because it's scientific. And you have to do it personably so that you get paid and invited back. That's the hard part. And it helps if you have a client who 'gets it'", he finished, nodding at Jeremy.

"Lol, I guess that's why I shouldn't be a contractor," said the new guy, turning to Alice with a self-deprecating smirk. "So, Alice, was Oz a Wonderland?"

Smiling faintly in return, Alice shook her head at the connection from her name to the book Alice in Wonderland where the main character also goes to Oz. "Clever. It was funny though. I was at the Boxing Day Test. Full of boozed-up Englishmen on the embankment."

"Ah, the Barmy Army."

"Yeah. I was sitting in the section adjacent to theirs with a friend and some workmates were joining us. They'd got to the section of the stadium we were in and were looking for us and one of them called out 'Alice!' The other one called out 'Alice!' almost at the same time. Then a thousand Englishmen yelled out 'Who the Fuck is Alice?'"

"Ah," said Tang, "from the song!"

"Yeah, I'd stood up to wave just before this happened, so it looked like I was admitting to being 'who the fuck was Alice'. I got a huge cheer. So the Barmy Army knew who I was after that."

"Fun times!"

Jeremy turned to Alice. "So, what do you want to do? More coding?"

Alice thought about this for a second. "I can *do* coding, but it's not what I'm born to do. I can do it, but... I'm not sure I'm all that good at it."

Barry looked mock shocked. "Aren't you putting the women's movement back? 'Girls can do anything' and all that?"

Alice shook her head "No. Women *can* do anything. I just don't know if *this* woman wants to do *that* thing. I just don't know if coding is my jam. The best coder I know is a woman. Actually, the *two* best are 10xers."

"Ten ex-ers?" Barry frowned at the unfamiliar term.

"Yeah, it's a marketing term. The theory is if you hire the best of the best, you pay twice as much, but they are 10 times as productive."

"And does that work out?"

"Well for those two it does— nice girls too. But I've been at places which have brought in the 10xers and oy vey! Sure, they ended up with someone who's better than your best existing employee, but they pissed off all the others with their arrogance and so everyone else ended up leaving. You get a surge in productivity, but then the 10xers get bored. They get a better offer and leave. Or, at the first downturn, they get cut because they're so expensive, and then nobody can support their code because it's written by a genius and they don't document any of it because documentation is beneath them. So as soon as you save all that money, your productivity dives and you start all over again." She paused for breath. "So, the takeaway is: do not hire arrogant geniuses."

"With the exception of your two friends."

She smiled "With the exception of my two friends. Actually, Troy are also 10xers, they just don't advertise themselves as that."

"Aw thanks," said Roy. "So Barry, what does it say on your business card then?"

"Funnily enough they don't allow me to have a business card, but on my email signature and employment contract it says I'm a Lead Behavioural Analyst."

"So does that mean you measure customer behaviour?"

"No."

"System behaviour?"

"No."

"Any behaviour?"

"No. I have nothing to do with behaviour in any way, shape or form."

"Oh... one of *those* sort of job titles..."

"Yeah, I guess I measure things so that management can make data-driven decisions."

"You sound like a guy with a ruler and a monocle."

"Lol," said Barry. Alice looked at him sharply. She'd never heard anyone actually say "lol", and now Barry had actually said it twice.

"So you do analytics," Tang offered.

"Yeah, I guess so," admitted Barry.

"See, that wasn't hard," muttered Dan.

The drinks after work were governed by a set of unspoken, unwritten rules. Presumably to keep trips to the bar to a minimum, when your glass was empty the practice was to see who else was almost empty and to buy a round for those about to finish. This usually evened out over time, with the number of rounds bought vs drinks received roughly equating, but it was easy to spot it when people exploited the rule for personal gain—those who ordered a more expensive drink when it was other people's turn to buy, or those who arrived consistently late so that they only had to pay for themselves, or those who could only stay for a number of rounds equal to one less than the number of people, ensuring that they would never pay. Those types were never invited back and when they did show up everybody would just leave rather than spend time with them. It was certainly possible to leave early or arrive later, as long as you admitted that it put you in an advantageous position with regards to buying a round, and you went out of your way to make it right. Stepping outside the "round buying" and only buying for yourself, for example—although that was considered rude if you did it without a reason. Nobody kept a ledger of every round missed or bought, but it was distinctly possible to see when someone was shirking. Knowledge of job openings was shared amongst those who stood their round, but no help was ever given to those who shirked.

This group never judged anyone for the drinks they ordered, though Alice had worked at a couple of places where the ale connoisseurs had looked aghast at anyone who didn't order the beer du jour (usually while stroking their well-oiled moustaches and riding a unicycle, but not at the same time) which of course changed faster than any other fashion trend. Not being the biggest drinker and being a woman of a slight build, Alice always stuck with half-pints of lager shandy, which meant that she was always coherent at the end of the evening, or as coherent as her drinking partners who tended to consume full pints of undiluted lager.

A round or two later she was fully caught up on the work front and had discussed the latest challenges each of them were facing. The conversation veered naturally from one topic to another until, for some reason, the topic of dating came up.

"Are you seeing anyone at the moment, Alice?" began Barry.

A little suspicious at the question, Alice allowed that, at the moment, she wasn't seeing anybody.

"I seem to find myself back in the dating pool," Barry continued. "It's been a little while but I'm throwing myself in there."

"Good for you," replied Alice, still suspecting that there was an ulterior motive to the line of conversation.

"So much so that I've gone on one hundred dates in the last three months."

"Oh! But that's..." Alice turned the numbers in her head. "That's like one every day for three months."

"Yeah, I've been pretty busy," agreed Barry. "But it's not quite one a night. Some weeks are lighter than others." He seemed falsely modest of the achievement and yet had been the one to bring it up.

"If some weeks have been lighter than others, some weeks must have been a lot busier than others. What was a busy week like?"

"Well, one a night on the weeknights, and then three each of the weekend days —one for lunch, one in the afternoon and one in the evening."

They all stared.

"Eleven in a week?" Alice was astounded.

"Oh, they weren't all first dates!" Barry said amused, and obviously enjoying the notoriety. "But it's a numbers game, right? You have to meet a lot of people to find ones who are good matches. And I met a lot of nice girls. Women. People. I met a lot of nice people."

"But how? And how did you keep them all separate in your mind? Did you make any mistakes? Call any of them the wrong name?"

"Oh, it's easy. Just say 'Hey, we could go backwards and forwards for a while and waste each other's time or we could just go out for a drink and see if we like each other.' They usually appreciated the honesty and the cutting-to-the-chase. I must admit there was one time I got caught misremembering someone as having a brother when she only had sisters but, by and large, I was pretty good. And after three or four dates with one person, I'd dial down the number of women I was seeing and see how that one panned out."

"But weren't you already seeing someone? What was her name? Janice? Jemima?"

"Janine? Yeah. Funny story there. Well, funny now, but at the time it was a bit annoying. I couldn't figure it out. So, we had been going out as boyfriend and girlfriend for a little while and she was showing me something on her screen at home, and I just happened to notice an email on her browser before she navigated away and one line in the middle of the email sprung out at me. 'It's a pity about Barry.' So, nothing concrete there, right? But then we were in bed and I had to get up early to go into the office and, as I came back from the bathroom to say goodbye, her phone flashed with an incoming message and showed part of the preceding message, and it said something like 'he's not a real man, not like you.' So I'm like… o…k… And before I leave, I ask her if she still wants to go out with me. And she looks up at me and says 'yes'. But later on, she texts me and says it's over. But why not break up with me that morning? I already knew it was over."

Alice looked him up and down. "You were standing over her when she was in bed? And you expected her to break up with you while she was lying in bed? You're a big guy. She had no way of knowing if you'd be violent or not—of course she's not going to break up with you like that."

Barry nodded. "I guess not. Still…"

"Yeah, I know. It's not nice finding out you're the only person invested in the relationship, right?"

"Yeah, and another weird thing. She had a very attractive friend, and we'd all sit outside in the sun and chat about this and that, and then Janine would find some excuse to head inside. I'd go in to see what she was up to, and she'd insist I stay outside talking to her friend. So, I'd head back out and chat. All very innocent and upfront. And the friend would chat along as well, but it always felt like they were waiting for something. Like a flirtatious remark or something. Or maybe me asking the very attractive friend out. And they always seemed disappointed that I never did. Strange."

Things petered out not long after that, with Jeremy promising to keep an eye out for coding work for her, and then leaving for the train with Troy. Barry headed home in a different direction, leaving Alice to retrace her steps back along Clerkenwell Road. She stopped in at the corner store to pick up a few things for dinner, getting home about 7pm.

Alice's cousin Zoltan had a large studio apartment on the edge of the

Barbican and was letting her stay there until she could find a place of her own. He was ten years older than Alice and there was family speculation about why he hadn't yet settled down with someone. Nobody could decide whether or not he was somehow stuck in the closet. Other cousins had come out and been accepted, so the Aunties (the cabal of elder female relations) could not figure out his situation. Alice could see them thinking the same about her in five to ten years.

Alice was in two minds about the Barbican. It'd taken her the full week to stop getting lost in the walkways and tunnels, and she now knew her way around. Previous attempts to help people navigate the skyways included drawing coloured lines on the pavements, and the remnants of the faded paint did go some way to directing people to where they wanted to go. Except when certain gateways were closed for renovations. And then you had to double back on yourself to find an exit.

As a thank you for letting her stay with him rent-free, Alice would periodically cook dinner for Zoltan or do laundry. The couch she slept on was incredibly uncomfortable, but she found if she wriggled into the gap between the back and the seat cushions, she could avoid the more uncomfortable springs and get some sleep. The Venetian blinds didn't do much to block the light through the floor-to-ceiling windows so she used the sleeping mask from the amenity kit given out on her flight over. Zoltan was sometimes out to all hours, but was home when she got in. She asked him if he'd eaten and when he said that he had not, she put a pot of water on and made some pasta and a salad. They chatted about the job hunt and Zoltan seemed impressed by the additional efforts Alice was taking—especially with her plans for the next day and the Soho lead.

"That would be so convenient!" he said, before realising that it would only be convenient if she was still at the Barbican—not nearly as convenient if she had to find a place to live further afield.

Alice checked her phone and it looked like Danica had indeed texted her the address and a time, so tomorrow was all set. She chatted a bit more with Zoltan and watched a bit of TV with him before getting changed for bed in the bathroom and climbing into the couch with a book. She felt drained after her afternoon of socialising. While she wasn't 100% introverted, she always found it exhausting being in those sorts of situations. She wasn't surprised that she found it very easy to slip into a slumber once the lights went out.

THE CLUB

A few hours later and a few hundred metres further down the road, Ingenue and her friend Sharleen were heading to a club. Ingenue was celebrating—her very first movie was coming out, and the advance reviews were looking very favourable. The Hollywood retelling of the events during The Insurrection, which had happened a few years earlier, was helped by the backstory of her own adventures hiding out in a bunker while chaos reigned over the Sussex countryside. The plot played a little fast and loose with the facts, and the love story had been slathered on pretty thickly, but it looked like enough time had passed since the events to get away with using them as backdrop to a romance rather than a raw scab on the psyche of the nation. There was even talk about possibly getting the nod for a Bafta.

She pulled up to the carpark outside Flannel, a retro 90's nightclub where the staff wore plaid shirts wrapped around their waists and the DJ's played remixes of classic rock. It was balancing on the edge between cutting and bleeding edge, with the it-crowd alternately lauding it as the next big thing and tearing it down as already being "over". Ingenue just wanted to dance—to blow off some steam. All she'd drink was water, which was the reason she was able to drive there, parking her Audi TTS Coupe with the Tango metallic red exterior, getting the ticket from the parking machine and placing it on the dash.

Greg the bouncer was sitting on the stool beside the velvet rope. He was black, over 6 foot tall, impressively muscled, dreadlocked, and heavily tattooed. Ingenue knew him from before she'd become halfway famous, so she paused for a while to chat.

"Slow night?" she asked, nodding to the empty queue.

He looked up and gave her a hug. "Sweetie, great to see you! I've been watching you! You're a star! Watch out Hollywood!"

"You're very kind," she allowed. "How's Trevor?"

"Third anniversary last month. That's twenty-one in gay years. I swear I could strangle that man."

"Congratulations!" Ingenue could never tell if his complaints about his partner were serious and that they were constantly on the verge of breaking up, or if they were a bickering odd couple who would be together forever, complaining about each other even in the rest home. "This is Sharleen," she said, indicating her friend who was staring unabashedly at the bouncer.

"*Enchantée*, madam," he said, bowing over Sharleen's hand. Sharleen giggled and held his hand a second longer than she needed to. He was a very attractive man.

They left the club about 4am, drenched in sweat and glowing from a three-hour aerobic workout. The explosion of flashes started as soon as Ingenue's foot hit the pavement outside the club and the night streetscape was illuminated as if it was daytime. A fairly impressive scrum of paparazzi were camped out on the road between the club and the carpark, ignoring a taxi trying in vain to get through.

Ingenue reached back and grabbed Sharleen's hand and they ran towards the car, paparazzi in tow. When they got to the carpark entrance, Ingenue stopped dead in her tracks. The cars parked on either side of hers had parked so close that there was no room for her to open either the driver or the passenger doors.

"Fuck, I knew I should have got the Roadster! Quick, back to the club!" They retraced their steps and Greg let them back in.

"That was unlucky," said Sharleen, as they caught their breath in the foyer. Outside, Greg was berating the photographers who'd followed them en masse back to the club.

"Hmm..?" answered Ingenue.

"Well, if only one person had accidentally parked so close we could have climbed in the other."

Ingenue glanced over at Sharleen. She'd been friends since high school but hadn't been around during the last seven years while Ingenue had been climbing the acting ladder, so she hadn't been exposed to the "high life".

"Oh honey, it's no accident. Those two cars will belong to the paps."

"But... Why would they do that? That's a bit mean."

'Well," replied Ingenue, choosing her words carefully, "worst case it means that we can't leave, so they get more photos of us. Best case would be that it's 4am and we've been drinking all night so we're tired and emotionally distraught and so they get photos of us crying."

Ingenue looked at Sharleen. Her friend back with disbelief. "That's not even the worst..." Ingenue continued. "Over in the States some of the stars have bought these huge industrial-sized trucks to guarantee that they can get away and not get boxed in."

"Oh no! Why do they do all these bad things?"

"The tabloids pay a lot of money for the pictures. So, if you've got no other skills and you can put your self-respect to one side, you can make some decent money. Some of my colleagues carry the same clothes so the only photos taken of them are all in the same outfit. It devalues the photos."

"Wow. Would anyone buy the magazines if they knew?"

"Are you kidding? Nobody cares: 'Poor little rich girl. Look at the pretty girl crying because she can't get into her Audi'. They could put it on a billboard or make a reality show on the shit that they pull, and nothing would change." Ingenue could feel herself getting angry but got her breathing under control and forced herself to be calm.

"But you know what? Not tonight. Fuck that shit." Sharleen watched as she pulled out her phone and unlocked it. "Not tonight."

A little while later Greg popped his head back inside to check up on them.

They let him know that they were fine, and he apologised for not warning them about the ambush. Ingenue let him know he wasn't to blame, and that she should have texted to see if the coast was clear. "I mean, it is Monday night, right?"

They waited another thirty minutes or so, chatting quietly to each other. Sharleen was the first to notice something change. It was like a wave of noise building up outside. Greg was stationed just inside the door of the club now and he started to get up when they approached but Ingenue waved him back down. They opened the door, poked their heads through and stared.

When Ingenue had time to think about it later, she managed to get a coherent view of what happened. At the time she just stood staring at the scene as it erupted.

The swarm of paparazzi had behaved like a beehive, flowing after her and Sharleen as they had run from club to carpark and back. Like a hive mind—a multitude of bodies with a single controlling entity. She knew that this wasn't actually the case, but their behaviour certainly followed that pattern. When enough of the paps were in the same place, some would split off and find secondary entrances to the club or hotel. In reality, Ingenue knew that this was because they'd each made an economic decision to give up the high chance of having a duplicate photo that all the other photographers would get in favour of the smaller chance of taking a unique photo if the star escaped out of a back door. But to her it seemed the hive mind entity controlling them all was just re-deploying their resources.

Looking outside, the illusion of coherence was dashed as the scrum of photographers were smashed by a gang of hoodie-wearing youths. The volume of noise swelled into a cacophony of screaming, swearing and smashing as the group broke apart to flee in every direction. The street only went in two directions though, so even as the paps collected themselves and tried to get away, a second group of dark hoodie-wearers met them from the other end.

The Hoodies body-checked the escaping paps, blocking their path and ripping cameras off their shoulders. It wasn't a brutal beatdown—while the Hoodies had baseball bats, they weren't trying to cause bodily harm to the paps and focused their attention on destroying the cameras. It didn't take much to break them—a lot were damaged from simply being dropped or kicked rather than destroyed with the bats, but the Hoodies were meticulous with finishing the job once they'd fallen to the ground.

Having said that, where there was resistance, it was brutally suppressed. If a Hoodie was pushed away, his cohorts descended with sickening speed on the guy who had pushed him. The violence was hypnotic, and Sharleen was getting very caught up in it, leaving the safety of the door to the club and cheering the Hoodies on. She even got out her phone to record the action. Ingenue didn't notice this until too late. She opened her mouth to shout a warning, but one of the Hoodies had heard the commotion of the cheering, looked over, seen the phone recording the action and, before the words could leave Ingenue's mouth, he'd lunged and smashed the phone out of Sharleen's hand. Pausing only to give the phone two hammer swings with his baseball bat and totally obliterating it, he moved on swiftly without a backwards glance.

Greg came out and helped Ingenue get Sharleen to her feet.

"Are you OK, Sharleen?" he asked.

"I'm OK now," she replied, staring up at him. Ingenue rolled her eyes.

"Nothing serious then?" she asked, a pointed edge to her voice.

"Oh, no," Sharleen managed, paying attention to Ingenue again. "Nah, I'm good."

"OK, we should probably get out of here before the cops show up."

Greg glanced over at that, but before he said anything Ingenue had grabbed Sharleen by the shoulder and headed towards her car, thanking Greg over her shoulder for his help. And telling him to say Hi to Trevor for her.

The cars that had surrounded hers had gone but, in their haste, one of them had left an ugly scrape down her driver-side door. Ingenue stood looking at it for a few minutes, practising her breathing techniques, before getting in and heading out into the just-awakening London Tuesday morning.

CRIME SCENE

Boris ducked under the scene tape and breathed deeply. The air had a soft coolness, the sky clear and promising another scorching hot day. The slight scent of a nearby Subway baking the morning's bread wafted past teasingly, and the morning chorus warbled softly in the background. Boris surveyed the scene.

The street was strewn with camera parts, a pair of scene examiners photographing the evidence before bagging and logging each piece. Boris was in reasonably good shape considering the number of years behind the desk. He was of average height and had been considered good looking in his prime due to a youthful appearance and easy smile. That had helped in questioning suspects back then, but the years of seeing the worst of humanity had taken its toll—the easy smile came just a little less easily, and the dark brown hair was now speckled with grey and the natural rapport had been replaced by a more cynical, knowledgeable insight into where and when to prod.

The immediate area containing the remnants of that morning's violence was marked off with yellow tape reading "CRIME SCENE—DO NOT ENTER". Further away, the blue and white tape marked with "POLICE LINE DO NOT CROSS" at each end of the street was beginning to attract clumps of office-bound workers, their routes to work blocked and their ability to navigate alternate routes to their offices stymied.

"Probably pre-coffee," he thought wryly as he approached the uniformed officer at one end who was explaining that no, they couldn't pass through while the Police were collecting evidence, as a serious incident had happened.

"Constable, can you run another line of tape from there to over there by the pub? It'll guide people along the footpath and naturally around the back of the carpark building so that they don't all bunch up here and want to walk through the scene."

"Right you are, Sarge," Morrison said and scampered off with the roll of Police 'do not cross' tape. Boris got him to repeat the process at the other end of the street while he moved the looky-loos along and then rolled up his sleeves to help bag and tag the evidence. He wanted to get it all back to the station as quickly as possible to start digesting the vast quantities of memory cards and hard drives that they had found. Plus, on top of all that, they still had to get all the CCTV footage from the cameras nearby. Boris stretched and breathed in the awakening city again, knowing that he'd be spending very little of the rest of the day outside in the fresh air.

Back at the station, the team got to work on the case.

"Hey Ford, did you get all the image files ghosted off the memory cards yet?"

"Not yet—we've got over two hundred of them."

"Well, how far through are we?"

"Almost there, but..."

"Yeah, I know, these things take time." Boris let him get back to it and returned to his desk. Whenever electronic media was involved, whether hard drives or memory cards, if you plugged them into a computer to read what was on them it actually changed the data. The "last viewed date" would obviously be changed and if you needed a particular piece of information that had been changed just from plugging it in to make your case and the defence lawyers found you hadn't followed protocol, forget about getting your conviction. So, the cards and hard drives were "ghosted"—an exact copy was taken by matching the 1s and 0s on the physical item using a special machine called a write-blocker, which would then lock the data so that it forensically stayed the same regardless of how many times they looked at the files.

"Morrison, do we have any victims yet? I saw a bunch of blood splatters—did we get DNA swabs from those? Any hospitals reporting injuries consistent with this incident?" Morrison went to find out.

"Graves, how are we doing for video footage? What time did the calls come in?"

"999 calls started at 4:57am, a few more following. I've got the CCTV from the club and the carpark over the road, plus I've logged the request for TFL at the stations." TFL was Transport for London—the local governmental body that ran the buses and underground stations and operated all the cameras in and around the stations. The carpark footage went to a central shared server and the Police had an arrangement with the company for quick access. The club had handed over their footage while Boris had been on site.

"Cool, show me what you've got."

They sat in one of the side offices with the shades pulled. On the screen in front of them, the two cameras showing the street were cued up to 4:50am. One showed the street alongside the entrance to the club, while the other pointed the other way along the pavement. The street showed the now-familiar sight of destroyed cameras, flashguns and lenses. Graves hit the rewind button and the street came alive with dozens of men jogging backwards and picking up all the camera parts. As the file continued to rewind, first one hoodie-wearing group and then another washed across the viewpoint like waves and disappeared, leaving the photographers in a huddle in the middle of the street on the edge of the CCTV view. They meandered there for quite a while, sped up like a Benny Hill chase scene, before surging towards the club entrance and then departing off-camera pursued by two stunning young ladies. Boris noted the time stamp as the paparazzi chased them back into the club immediately after.

"So, we've got a—what, a mass mugging of a bunch of paparazzi after the two society ladies try to leave the club?"

"Nope: nothing stolen. Let's watch it in real-time."

Going forward in real time allowed them to focus on the exact moment that the Hoodies arrived, what time they fled, and what time the ladies had left and returned to the club. They then went back even further, noting what time the paps had begun to arrive.

"OK, so I make it 2:27am that the first photographer arrives. They're all there by 3:40am. The ladies—can you make out who they are? No? Whoever they are, they leave at 4:03, and by 4:07 they're back at the club. The first group of Hoodies arrive at 4:45, the ones from the other side five minutes later. One of the ladies gets assaulted at 4:53. The Hoodies are gone by 4:55, the ladies straight away after that and then we get the call from the club at 4:57."

"So, you need to get in touch with the club and ask them who was on that night. Who or what attracted the paps?"

"Cool: will do. And here is the carpark coverage. I'll start at 5:00am." The camera footage was black and white and not quite as fine a resolution as the club's coverage, but they could see the departure of the Audi, complete with gash down the side.

"Oh dear," managed Graves, deadpan. He hit rewind.

Moments later they saw the paps' cars leave in a hurry.

"Wow, that was some tight parking—but there's heaps of space on either side."

"I don't think that was an accident—keep going back."

They watched the arrival times of Ingenue and subsequently the paparazzi who parked either side, noting the times and comparing the timestamps between cameras.

"Hmm... so we have our lady friends running from the club, discovering that they're boxed in and returning to the club. Thirty minutes later our friends in the Hoodies turn up and all hell breaks loose. Nothing stolen, just the cameras broken. Bit of a coincidence don't you think?"

Without waiting for an answer, Boris changed tack. "Any word from the club?"

"They're not saying anything: quoting customer privacy."

"Ask them how many customers they will have if we have to shut them down because of the fights going on outside their club."

Graves headed out to make the call.

Graves came back a few minutes later, smiling.

"It was Ingenue."

"The actress? Interesting! Can someone track her down and get her in for questioning? How are we going with collating and sorting those images?"

"Got the pics all downloaded chief but it's going to take a while to go through them all. Like a long time."

"Shit, how many pictures are we talking about?"

"They're paparazzi: there are *terabytes* of pictures."

"Terabytes? What's that, bigger than kilobytes?" Boris had been accused of being a Luddite for not having upgraded his phone for the past five years, and so enjoyed playing the part, deliberately getting terminology wrong in conversation with the team and pretending ignorance on current technology.

"Heh, Sarge. Yeah, there's thousands of photos here, maybe hundreds of thousands."

"Bloody hell, what do they do, sit there with their finger on the shutter the whole time? Why don't they just take a video? When can the tech guys get to it?"

"They said September."

Boris stared at him.

"Seriously, they're backed up!"

"Shit. OK, let's think about alternatives." Boris rubbed a hand over his face. "Coffee?"

"Sure—Starbucks?"

"I guess so," Boris responded, heading to the door.

THE STATION

Danica was starting to get upset.

"Well, what else are you going to do?" she demanded.

"I've taken your report, madam, and as soon as an officer becomes available and is in a position to investigate the case, then they will do so," the officer behind the window said.

"I don't think you're taking this seriously at all!"

"Oh, no, ma'am. The Malicious Communications Act 1988 section 1 is pretty clear that this is a serious offence. I have your details, and as soon as an officer becomes available, I'm sure they will be in touch if they need anything further."

"And when will that be?"

"I'm afraid I don't know the answer to that question."

"You have been no help at all. Let's go, Alice," said Danica, turning to leave.

A couple of officers, one uniformed and one not, chose that time to exit the police station too, spoiling Danica's exit flounce as she had to pause and allow them to leave the station first.

Alice and Danica followed them out of the station, inadvertently overhearing their conversation—something about trying to look through thousands of images and finding a needle in a haystack.

Alice cleared her throat.

"I might be able to help you out," she offered.

They turned and looked at her. The uniformed one was about her age, average height and thin build. The other, in jeans and a collared shirt under a pullover, was a little taller and middle-aged. She had their attention.

"I know a guy who built software for categorising images of people," she offered.

"No way, really?" responded the younger, uniformed one.

"That would solve our problem, but even if you can do what you say you can do, we can't just trust anyone who we bump into at a police station. We have no idea who you are," said the older man.

Alice held out her hand. "I'm Alice Woodstock," she began. "Before I moved to Australia, I did some contract work in the defence industry and had to get Security Clearance and Deeply Vetted. Would that be enough?"

"I'm Detective Sergeant Boris McDonald, this is Constable Denver Graves."

"SC and DV? That would tick that box, Sarge," added Graves.

Seeing Alice's confused look, Boris explained. "We have a special form for taking on external consultants and we've got to establish the bona fides of anyone doing work for the force. There's a special box for background checks and having DV means I don't have to get my Inspector to sign it off. So, it looks like we can accept your help after all."

"But," she said, seeing that they were sold, "you've got to help my friend out." She nodded towards Danica.

"What's the problem?"

"Dick pics."

Boris looked apologetic. He shook his head at Alice.

"Look, even after you get evidence of telling some guy to stop and he still carries on, hunting him down and then getting a conviction is a low probability case, but we could really use your help on the categorising piece."

Alice stood firm. "If it's worth something to you maybe you could look into the sexually explicit pictures being sent to my friend?"

Boris' eyes twinkled and he relented. "Look, no promises, but if you help us out, I'll do what I can to get someone to have a look at your dick pics."

Graves piped up. "Assuming she helps us out, what about 'chain of evidence'?"

Boris nodded thoughtfully, mentally going through the other checkboxes on the form in his head. "Well, we've ghosted the memory cards which takes an exact copy without affecting them."

That was apparently a good enough answer for the younger officer, who continued: "What about privacy?"

The older one turned to Alice. "They won't keep the images, will they? They'll delete them straight away, right?"

"I'll check," she said, taking out her phone.

She rang a number and then left a message. "Fabian, Alice. Give me a ring."

As soon as she hung up, her phone rang.

"Hi. Yeah, that was me. Do you still have your... face recogniser website up?"

She glanced over at Boris and reddened slightly.

"Yeah, that one. Any chance of sending me a login?" A pause. "Awesome, thanks..." More listening, and then, "Hang on. Two questions. Does it keep a copy? The images—do they persist on the site? No? OK. And who did you train the algorithm on?" She listened carefully, thanked him again and then hung up.

She smirked a little. "Fabian is really into South Asian porn, but he's sick of the miscategorisation of pictures so he built a site which would go through a folder of porn and sort the actresses into subfolders."

Boris looked nonplussed. "I don't care about that," he said

"You should—he trained the algo on Bollywood stars."

"OK...?" he offered, not seeing the problem.

"So, facial recognition learns from what you feed into it. If you give it faces from the subcontinent, it won't be very good at recognising black or white faces."

"Ah," he said, getting it at last. "So we can't be 1000% sure of matches in the results and therefore we shouldn't use what we find for arresting people, just for further questioning." He nodded, coming to a conclusion. "I think we have a deal."

Alice grinned and shook his hand.

An hour later, all one hundred and seventeen thousand photos from the seventy-three memory cards recovered were categorised and logged by Fabian's website. The resulting page had catalogued the individuals involved and had the clearest photo as a profile picture for each of them.

Most of the pics of the hoodie-wearing hoodlums were blurred or partial at best, leaving them without any leads. Graves had tried to go back through the paparazzis' earlier photos, that were taken before the attack, but Boris had pulled him up short with a quiet word and one eye on Alice. "We've got enough on our plate." Using the photos of the attack was an acceptable use of evidence but if they found anything else they could be accused of fishing for other crimes.

Going through the photos of the hoodie-wearers, most of them were barely distinguishable from each other except by shade or brand of tracksuit or slight variation in height or stature, the markings on walls in the background being used as reference points to establish their heights. Alice was impressed at the lengths Fabian had gone to in order to identify, differentiate and catalogue the adult actresses. Porn was truly the cutting edge of technology.

"We don't have enough of a match to identify a face, but we might be able to get a match on this tattoo," Boris said, tapping the screen in front of them.

Alice glanced at her phone. "Oh, shit, I'm going to be late." Danica had headed off straight away to meet her contact in Soho, telling Alice she'd try to set up a lunch with them afterwards to allow Alice to meet them and wow them with her ability. Danica was impressed at her friend's support in getting the pictures investigated so was going out of her way to help in the job search, but Alice still had to get from the station to Soho in time for the lunch, so she had to hustle.

"Give me a call when you're ready for the photos to be deleted," she said, writing her number on a Post-it note. "I'll get all the images deleted securely, so make sure you've done everything you need to before you ring though. Otherwise, you'll have to upload them all over again!"

"No problem—thanks again for your help."

The tattoo was distinctive—a tribal glyph with a reference to a south London postcode, and it wasn't long before the computer system had a hit.

The next day, Boris was sitting opposite the tattooed individual and his very well-dressed lawyer from one of the Magic Circle law firms. Graves sat beside him and frowned slightly at the difference in clothing between the lawyer and his client.

Graves hit the record button on the machine on the desk and read from an aide-memoire, although in truth he could probably have done it purely from memory. "This interview is being tape-recorded and may be given in evidence if your case is brought to trial." Adding which interview room in which police station they were in, the date, the time, Graves's name and rank, Boris's name and rank, the solicitor's name. Leaving a pause for Noah to state his name and date of birth before reminding him he was entitled to free and independent legal advice and, finally, reading the caution.

"Thanks for helping us with our enquiries, Noah." A smirk had flashed across his face when the preamble had mentioned the free and independent legal advice.

Noah started to answer but the lawyer spread his fingers on the desk. Noah noticed and shut his mouth and the lawyer responded.

"We're happy we can help with your enquiries, Constable. Mr Watson and I have both got other engagements this afternoon so could we get to the meat of the matter please?"

"Of course! We have some photos we'd like for you to see, Noah," Graves continued, spreading two photos out on the desk. "Multiple counts of

Criminal Damage occurred in the early hours of yesterday morning outside a nightclub in Farringdon. We managed to get this from one of the victim's cameras. One of the perpetrators looks to have a tattoo very much like the one on your left arm."

Boris noticed Noah move his right hand to cover the place on his left arm where the tattoo was, even though he was wearing a windbreaker that hid it.

"My client has indeed got a tattoo on his left arm, and it may well look a lot like the tattoo on the photo, but he's not alone in having this tattoo."

"I wouldn't call the tattoo a common one—it's not like a heart with Mum on it, right? It's quite specific to your neighbourhood in South London, isn't it Noah?'

Noah looked at the lawyer who nodded. Something was wrong here, thought Boris. When you bring boys like Noah in for questioning, first of all it's the devil of a job finding them and then when you do get them in a questioning room, they sweat buckets and you either can't get them to talk or else they're full of piss and vinegar and angry abuse. This guy was... calm. And he'd come into the station as soon as he heard that they were looking for him. And *him.* He looked at the lawyer. Top firm. Senior, not an Associate, so huge billable hours. What the hell was he doing representing Noah? This smelled bad. Really, really bad.

"Me and the massive got the same tatt, bruv."

"So, all your gang—friends," Graves hurriedly corrected himself after a glance from the lawyer, "have the same tattoo? Do you know where they all were yesterday morning?"

"I'm afraid we can't answer questions about where other people were, officers, only where my client was. And he was in bed at his grandmother's house in Brixton."

"So, if the man in the photo is not you, could it possibly be someone in your... massive? Do you recognise them?" asked Graves.

Noah leant over and made a show of looking at the photo, trying a few angles before handing it back and shaking his head. "Nah, bruv, could be anyone, init?"

To be fair, the photo *was* grainy, only a minuscule part of the person's face was showing and there weren't any landmarks in the background for establishing the subject's height in the shot. Asking for an ID was a stretch.

Graves looked over at Boris, the glance indicating that he'd exhausted his questions. After a thoughtful pause, Boris nodded.

"Do you wish to add anything further or to clarify any point or anything you have told me?" asked Graves.

Synchronized head shakes. "No."

Graves slid a form over to the solicitor. "Here is a notice which explains the entitlement to a copy of the tapes used in this interview."

The solicitor barely looked at it before signing it.

Graves continued in a monotone, stating that the interview was concluded and giving the date and time.

Boris put both hands on the desk and stood up.

"Thanks for coming in and for your time—both of you. Very refreshing." Graves led them out, Noah first, and just before the lawyer left the room, Boris asked him for a word.

"I have reason to believe that young Noah there is caught up in something a lot bigger than he is and that, if that's the case, he's paying your fee with funds obtained illegally."

The lawyer coolly responded. "I'm fully aware of my responsibility regarding the legality of funds used to pay my firm's fee and am satisfied that they come from legitimate sources." He paused. "If there's nothing else, Sergeant?"

Boris pursed his lips and wordlessly held the door open for him, watching as he collected Noah in the reception area and headed out the door.

He met Graves back at their desks.

"Well, that was a dead end. If we pick our man Noah up later, he'll just lawyer up again. Can we look at one of his homies? Any weak links there?"

Graves didn't answer for a while—looking at the floor with a frown on his face.

"...Graves?"

"Sarge, where was the lawyer from?" he eventually asked.

Boris told him.

"That's what I thought. When we were waiting for him at the end there, Noah got out his phone. You know just before you unlock it, you can see all your notifications? Well, I managed to catch a glimpse of his phone screen. There were a bunch of notifications with 'TapPaps-Lawyer' as the contact. Now, surely you would have had the legal firm's name there? Or maybe just 'Lawyer'. Or a description like 'Dickhead'."

"So, what the hell is 'TapPaps' then?"

"Now *that's* the million-dollar question."

TAPPAPS

"Hi, Alice, Sergeant Boris McDonald here."

"Oh, hi Boris, I'm assuming it's ok to delete all the photos? How's it going?"

"Yeah, we've hit a bit of a brick wall, actually. We managed to trace the people to a website called TapPaps, but we don't have any credentials to access the site and we're coming up blank on who owns it." Boris had uncharacteristically let a trace of frustration into his voice.

The tapping in the background turned out to be Alice on the laptop.

"So, you need to find everything about this website?"

"Have you got it up there? Yeah, we've figured out who's hosting it but it's going to take a few days to get a warrant to get the client details from the hosting company. They've got Privacy turned on for the domain to protect against spam, which makes it an extra step to get those details. Even then, there's every chance it'll be a prepaid credit card and a rubbish company name."

Alice was silent.

"Are you there? Sorry to lay all this on you. I thought you'd be interested in our progress and that you might be able to tell us something about—"

"I know who made this!" Alice interrupted, staring at her laptop in disbelief.

"Say that again?"

Alice continued. "So, if you View Source in your browser to see the code behind the website, sometimes the developer puts some detail in there—a copyright notice, an author tag or meta tags which identify them as the person who wrote the code."

"OK..." Boris prompted.

"So, when you make websites for a living, you create a sign-in page and an admin section and then just reuse that for each site. Build it once and reuse it. And this guy I know called Mike—Morocco Mike we call him, really nice guy—" Alice could sense Boris' impatience. "Anyways, in his boilerplate section that he reuses on all his sites, he has comments indicating that he wrote the site. And that's what I'm looking at now."

"Is it possible that someone else coincidentally has come up with the same comments?"

"Sure, anything is possible, but I think it's really unlikely. And their name would have to be the same as Mike's. And their nickname would have to be Morocco Mike. And they'd have to be making the same off-colour joke as well."

"Ah, OK. So, not likely a coincidence. This is great. How do I get in touch with Mike?"

"I have a phone number for him, but no address and there's no address on the site. How about I ring him and ask him to get in touch?"

Boris paused, weighing up whether it was better to have a friendly voice encouraging Mike to get in touch, or whether he'd get better results going direct.

"If you tip him off and he flees, then our case hits a dead-end, so how about you ask about it but don't mention the case. And I'll need his full name and address. We don't want this sort of violence to be repeated, so we've got to lock this TapPaps website down ASAP."

"OK, I won't spook him. I'll find out where he is."

Mike answered straight away.

"Hi Alice, how are things in Oz? What time is it there anyways?"

"Heh, I'm back in London—I came back."

"What, got sick of the perfect weather?"

"Something like that. How're things going with you?"

"I'm actually emigrating too—going to head overseas for a while."

"Oh, where to?"

"Haven't decided yet. I'm actually at the airport now, deciding."

"Sudden decision? Is this because of one of your sites, TapPaps?"

"TapPaps? Yeah, that was me."

He didn't seem bothered by the question at all. Alice paused. Boris hadn't wanted her to spook Mike, but it looked like he was already on the way out. Alice figured she'd need to get as much as she could from Mike— just in case he totally disappeared.

"Hey look, I'll come clean, the police want to know some more information about the guys who got you to make it—you're not in any trouble or anything."

It was Mike's turn to pause. She continued.

"I can talk to the guy in charge and see about getting you some sort of immunity."

"Ah," said Mike eventually, "...that's not the reason I'm getting out of town."

"Huh?" said Alice.

"Are you sitting down? You need to sit down for this. So, you know how some clients are ok with you working from home? Well, towards the end of TapPaps, they said they wanted me to work from their offices. It's the last week of the contract, most of it is done, a little rework, one or two little bugs. No problem. Above a shop opposite the British Museum. I take my laptop and headphones along and meet the client. Two gym-bunny muscle guys in suits with buzz cuts. When they say 'Hello', they've got heavy Russian accents. I can't stop myself and blurt out, 'Are you guys Russian mobsters or something?' I'm joking, but they look kind of uncomfortable and I realise if they take it the wrong way I'm in trouble. I straight away resolve not to say anything the rest of the time I'm there. Which is not like me, right?"

"Right. If we didn't call you Morocco Mike, we'd call you Mr Sociable."

"Aww, thanks. Anyways, they led me down the hallway, three offices and a meeting room. I'm at the far end, the meeting room is beside me and then there are two other offices, closest to the kitchenette and the toilet. The other two offices have got guys in them doing some sort of coding work as well. I get my headphones on, crank the tunes and start working. No problem. They check in with me a couple of times during that first day and each time I'm in the flow and they have to nudge me to attract my attention. No problem. The next day I go in and they're not there. Cool, nod at the other guys as I pass their cubicles and get to work in mine. I kind of finish off all the work I can do and grab a cup of tea from the kitchenette. As I'm passing the last office, I notice that the guy working there has just put down his phone and he's obviously not in the middle of something so I ask him if he wants a cuppa as well. He says yes and when I bring it to him, I ask what he's working on. There's a soldering iron in his office and a whole lot of electronic components as well, so I'm thinking it's something boss. His name is Bart and he's doing a hardware interface for a remote-control car. I'm like 'huh?' And he's like, 'Well you know how the controller sends radio waves to the car which tells it what to do?' And I'm like, 'Well I do now'. He says, 'Well, I'm changing that so that it uses a cell phone connected to the internet to do all the controls and send a camera-feed back to the server'. 'Cool,' I say. Then he says that Tim, the guy in the next office, is doing a web front-end for it. So, you could sit anywhere in front of your computer and see what the remote-controlled car sees and control it. Cool tech! I go back to my office and do some work for a different client while I'm waiting for some changes to the TapPaps design that they're getting someone in the Philippines to do. It comes through eventually, so I get to work implementing the changes. I get up to grab another cup of tea and in walks the Russian bosses and some Arabic guys. I'm about to go over and say 'Salaam' when one of the Russian guys catches my eye and shakes his head. Like really subtly but holding my eye. So I shrug and make my tea and head back to my desk. I put my headphones on while I get the next playlist queued up. A few minutes later, I hear an argument from the meeting room—the two Arabic guys going at it in Emirati."

"Huh? What's Emirati?"

"So, Arabic isn't one language—each region has its own dialect. I speak Moroccan Arabic because I was born in Morocco."

"So how do you understand each other? Arabs who aren't from Morocco?"

"Well, if you speak High Arabic, then sure, we can follow each other, but nobody speaks that by choice, only when you've found a fellow Arabic speaker who doesn't understand your home dialect. It's like the way BBC broadcasters used to talk. All stilted and awkward. Emirati is the flavour of Arabic spoken in the United Arab Emirates and Kuwait."

"Oh..." Alice responded. "So how much could you understand?"

"Maybe 30%. They were talking about how effective something was, how the effort wasn't enough, how it was wasted. There was something about elegance and poetry that really pissed the other guy off. One thing I heard quite distinctly was 'Why don't you just make each of them have a bomb?'. That made me sit up. I didn't hear too much else after that. They shifted to English and the Russians must have come into the meeting room too because I could hear them talking. They kept talking about some guy named Scorpion, but that couldn't be right. First of all, it's the name you'd give to a bad Hispanic crime lord, right? El Scorpion. Second, they kept mentioning it as if there were many of them coming from Europe. Like a plague of insects or something. I kept my headphones on and pretended I was listening to music while working and, when they all left, one of the Russian guys popped his head around the corner and said something. I didn't hear him and when I said 'Hmm? What?' he grunted and went away. Week ended, I got paid in cash (which tells you they were dodgy), and I moved on to other clients."

"No more bugs or rework?"

"There were a few inconsequential changes and tweaks that they wanted, but they let me fix those remotely."

"OK, so what's the problem? Why are you fleeing the country so dramatically?"

"You know the body they found in that burned-out car?"

"On Saturday?"

"Yeah, in that industrial park. They found all sorts of drugs lying around outside the car—party drugs."

"Yeah, that guy."

"Yeah."

"Yeah, that was Tim—the guy from the next office doing the web front end for the RC car. I recognised him from the photos in the paper. Well, the 'before the fire' photos anyway. And that guy I spoke to? Bart? Yeah, he was found in a park. Needle in his arm. OD. So, whatever they were working on got them killed. I assume they'd finished up and the Russian guys were erasing their tracks. I've got some remote clients, so I've got work, but I'm getting the fuck out of town."

"Where will you go?"

There was silence. She could feel his stare through the phone. "Best you don't know. Best that nobody knows."

"Why don't you go to the cops?"

"The cops? Let's just say that there are a few other reasons why I might not want to come to the attention of our friends in blue."

She didn't want to pry, though she was dying to know what that meant.

"Well, best of luck, Mike," Alice said, the sadness evident in her voice.

"Thanks, Alice—stay safe."

Alice thought of something.

"Hang on, tell me more about this remote-control car website."

"Huh?" Mike didn't get it.

"Do you know who is hosting it?" she persisted.

"I don't know, I didn't even talk to Tim who was doing the front end. If it was anything like TapPaps, then I really can't help you there. I pushed the code to the Git repo and then gave them the password when they paid the final invoice. No clues there I'm afraid."

"Ok, thanks again for your help..." Alice didn't hear him hang up. She was staring into space, lost in thought. All this talk about bombs, and Arabs and Russians. Wondering how to unpick the puzzle, trying to piece everything together. Feeling a little lost.

Alice finally rang Boris, still mulling over what Mike had told her.

"Hi, Alice, what can you tell me? When can we speak to your friend Mike?"

"Uh... there's been a bit of a development. He's fled the country."

"Goddammit! What the hell did you say to him?"

"Look I can only tell you if you promise that Mike won't get in trouble."

"Alice, I can't promise that. All I can tell you is that I'm only following up on this lead for the bashing crime. I have no intention of following up on anything else I discover."

"Fine, but look, he was already on his way out of the country when I spoke to him." And then she told him what Mike had told her. Boris murmured when she told him about the office opposite the British Museum, so she surmised that he had learned of that through his other investigations.

Boris was silent.

"What's wrong? Do you know El Scorpion?"

"I... I can't discuss the particulars of the case," responded Boris slowly.

"Look, I've played fair with you, I've told you what I know and I didn't have to do that. I've given you all the leads you've needed. Why would I help you anymore, unless you share what you know?"

"OK." Another pause. "I guess it would be Los Skorpions, not El Scorpion."

"Huh? Some sort of Spanish gang?"

"No, it's many skorpions. A skorpion is a gun. With a k not a c. It's small calibre, incredibly easy to conceal and, more importantly, low recoil. We've had some reports from Interpol that certain Slavic underworld groups have come across a cache of these weapons and we've been keeping an eye out for them. We knew that there were a whole bunch of them and that they're so small, it's hard to pick them up. It looks like your friend Mike has tripped over a plot to put these skorpions onto RC cars and have them remotely controlled from a website."

"Who would do such a thing?"

"Terrorists. Or people who really hate ankles."

"Shit!" said Alice, ignoring the dark humour. "So how can you find out if the skorpions have been shipped here?" asked Alice.

A longer silence.

"I don't think that you can. I'll notify the organised crime guys and the anti-terrorism squads but tracking down a hundred RC cars and a hundred skorpion guns and ammo is like finding a needle in a haystack."

"What about the Russians' office? The one opposite the British Museum? Have you searched that for clues?"

"We'll go and get a warrant and have a look tomorrow. But if you're right and it's a rented office space, my expectations are low. The criminals are getting smarter and smarter. They're using encryption, they're getting secure communications. They're making their own criminal ecommerce sites for fuck's sake. It's suspicious as fuck if you buy 100 phones from a high street store... and you're not going to need high-end phones, are you? You're going to need a data plan and a barebones phone soldered into the car and attached to the gun and then the camera as well. Unless the phone includes the camera. Your man, Morocco Mole..."

"Morocco Mike," corrected Alice.

"Morocco Mike, didn't say anything about the model of phone, did he?"

She frowned at her phone in disbelief.

"I think we're lucky that he remembered the brand of remote-control car—let's not—"

"Ok, ok," responded Boris, conceding the point. "Well, with Amazon being everybody's storefront, we won't know where the assembly point is. Where they'll do the soldering and adding the bits together."

"Why not? Surely they can tell us the address which has taken delivery of 100 phones with cameras, 100 sim cards with a data plan and 100 RC cars?"

"Amazon will tell us to get fucked. Even if they would tell us, we don't have enough information to identify the deliveries we care about. Our ask is too broad, they'll claim, and the courts will agree, that we're fishing. The phone companies help us out with identifying prepaid customers, but only with walk-ups—customers that wander into one of their stores. A corporate order of a hundred phones doesn't have any ID requirements—no photo from a store security camera that we can add to the file. And a hundred RC cars getting delivered to a company called 'RC Cars Incorporated' doesn't raise any eyebrows. They're just stocking up all their retail stores. Perfectly innocent."

"So we're a bit stuck?"

"We'll see how we get on tomorrow, but yeah, one step forward, two steps back."

"Well, let me know if I can help," Alice said, genuinely wanting to be helpful.

"We'll let the pros have a look first and if they don't find anything, then who knows, maybe."

Alice couldn't figure out if he was patronising her or being genuine, hanging up before eventually deciding to give him the benefit of the doubt.

THE SCENE

It was midday the next day when Boris rang.

Alice had spent the morning doing job searches on the internet while sitting on the balcony overlooking the street below. The stacked balconies of the apartment block created a permanent shadow but the sun was so harsh she was glad of the protection. She kept glancing over at her phone, trying to tell herself that it was because of all the job applications that she was sending out, but she had to admit that was a lie when a recruiter rang her and she found herself disappointed that it wasn't Boris.

So, when he rang just before she was going to get something for lunch, she pounced on the phone.

"The scene guys have had a look."

"Did they find anything?" Alice tried to hide the eagerness in her voice.

"Nothing compelling—did you want to come and have a look?"

"Sure!"

He gave her the address of the office and she headed to the tube station. She grabbed a sandwich from the convenience store at the base of the stairs in the station before making the connection to the Central Line and emerging from Tottenham Court Road station, blinking in the midday sun.

She headed towards the British Museum, dodging a large group of Spanish high school students and an exasperated teacher haranguing them in rapid-fire Español. The address was for a large black door situated beside a Fish and Chip shop. The door was pinned open and a short corridor beckoned beyond. After stepping through the doorway, an opening immediately on the right revealed the interior of a convenience store, while the corridor continued on, ending at a staircase crisscrossed with police tape and guarded by a uniformed policeman. A tall Middle Eastern man—apparently the shopkeeper—beckoned her in and told her not to worry about the policeman. He bustled to his position behind the counter before looking disappointed that Alice hadn't followed him into his store. She smiled at him as she stepped past the opening and told the uniformed policeman that she was here to see Boris.

He called ahead on his radio and a few minutes later the door swung open and Boris beckoned her in. Beyond, a short hallway continued past some white stairs with cheap carpet heading both up and down. The stair was blocked by yellow tape. The uniformed officer handed Boris a clipboard and he filled in their names. Then Boris lifted the tape to allow Alice through and they headed up the stairs to the first floor.

Boris nodded back to the stairs. "Shopkeeper is Turkish, we've already got his security footage. English school out the back on the ground floor, music studio in the basement, empty apartment on the top floor. We've questioned them all—nothing out of the usual, they all remember seeing the Russians, but nothing stands out. No unusual deliveries or anything."

"What's the name on the rental agreement for the office?" she asked.

"It's a company name that does not exist. Rent received every month, so no alarm bells."

"Didn't the landlord do a background check or anything?"

"Apparently not. They're coming down with a key to the mailbox."

Boris opened the door to the office which proved to be empty of people. Alice had expected to see officers in jumpsuits, masks and hats so was a little taken aback that it was empty.

"Has everybody left?"

"Yeah, they didn't find anything—took some prints so we're expecting matches after they run them through the computer. Don't touch anything, but you can look around. We've got the contents of the rubbish and the

Forensics guys will go through that for anything interesting."

The door opened into a small reception area with a desk for a receptionist. Off the reception area was a kitchenette and a door emblazoned "Toilet". Opposite the kitchenette was a corridor running along the line of windows overlooking the street. Across from the windowed corridor were the offices and meeting room, each behind a glass wall—with a single desk and chair in the offices and a long table with four seats in the meeting room.

The offices weren't much bigger than the desks which were directly in front of the glass wall so that anyone passing in the corridor would not be able to see what was on your screen.

She headed to the end office where Mike would have been working.

As she expected, it was empty. Nothing written on the underside of the desk. Nothing down the back or side of the desk. Nothing at all.

The meeting room, Tim's office, and Barry's office were likewise devoid of anything of interest.

She turned and Boris was watching her.

"Forensics didn't find anything, either."

She went over to the window.

"That's the British Museum—is that relevant?" she said, inclining her head.

Boris nodded. "Yeah, I thought of that—I think they wanted the office because it was centrally located and/or cheap. If they were Greek instead of Russian—maybe. The Elgin Marbles are still there. It's also close to the Trades Union Council. But you can't really see either of them very well from these windows."

"Yeah, funny, eh?" Alice indicated the Museum across the road. "Who else puts all the antiquities that they've stolen on display in a purpose-built Museum? Like 'Here's all this stuff we looted. You can't have it back.'"

Boris smiled back.

"Well, it looks like you've covered everything. I'm not sure what else there is to find."

The radio on Boris's belt bleeped and he answered it, listening carefully.

"I'll pop down," he said into the radio. "Well, we tried," he said to Alice. "It was only on the off chance, just in case you came up with an insight that we missed."

"So, I shouldn't feel too bad?" Alice asked. Not really feeling bad at all.

"Nah, if you'd picked up something that the professionals missed, I'd have been surprised," he said.

They headed back downstairs to find the storekeeper yelling at a South Asian lady.

"It's against the law—it's a fire hazard!" he exploded.

"Mind your own business," she retorted, getting heated.

"Is there a problem here?" interjected Boris.

"They're blocking the emergency exit! The boxes and carpets! They're in the emergency exit. It's against the rules."

"It's none of your business, Hakan," the landlady said through gritted teeth.

"The carpet is coming away from the floor! It's a trip hazard!"

Boris stepped between the two of them, "I'm afraid all of those are local council issues. You'll have to take it up with them." His body blocked the doorway between the shopkeeper and landlady, who looked up at him with a little relief.

"I have the key to the mailbox here," she said, handing it to him but keeping an angry eye on the shopkeeper.

In the shared hallway before the inner door to the staircase stood a dark blue metal mailbox about waist high which had four equal-sized doors. Boris slipped latex gloves on and gripped the key carefully while unlocking the door. Inside, there was a mixture of envelopes and advertising pamphlets.

Boris had a plastic evidence bag out at the ready. He grabbed a handful of mail and placed it into the bag. The second handful was topped and tailed with advertising pamphlets. The combination of the latex gloves and the shiny paper made it impossible to grasp properly and most of the second handful spilled onto the floor.

Feeling bad that she hadn't been able to provide any assistance upstairs in the office, Alice bent down to help pick up the mail. Hearing Boris' sharp intake of breath she froze, remembering he'd said not to touch anything.

"Don't!" Boris managed, bending down and scrabbling for the mail. He collected it all and safely secured it into the bag.

Still frozen in a crouch, Alice noticed that tucked under the edge of the carpet was the corner of a card.

"What's that?" she asked, pointing. Boris pulled the frayed and badly attached carpet away from behind the mailbox and examined the two or three items hidden there.

"Postcards: dental reminder for the flat above, courier card for the basement studio, and... bingo! 'Thanks for signing up to SpareSpace.com'— addressed to our friends upstairs."

Alice felt elated!

Boris continued, turning the card over in his hands. "Dated a week ago. Who the fuck are SpareSpace?"

Alice pulled her phone out and within seconds was reading out the advertising content on the home page of their site.

"SpareSpace fills last minute availability transportation options... Green efficiency... Save the planet... Lower the carbon footprint... blah blah... sunk costs, pollution. Maximise usage... Unmanned drop-offs allowed."

Noticing that the landlady was taking an interest in the conversation, Boris indicated that they should leave. He handed the key back to the landlady, thanking her, giving her a business card and telling her if there was any more mail for the office to let him know.

As they left, he turned to Alice. "Can you find us a phone number for this SpareSpace?"

"Yup, it's right there on the site."

SPARESPACE

The SpareSpace offices were very conveniently located in Holborn. After about an hour navigating the switchboards and being bounced from one disinterested party to the next, they managed to communicate the importance of a meeting and had an appointment to meet the CEO and his legal team.

Given the eco-friendly language on the website, Alice expected the offices to be similar to the ones they'd just left, so she was a little astounded to find them on the main road and taking up a whole floor of a four-level office block. The building had floor-to-ceiling windows and a shared reception area with security turnstiles, complete with security guard. The décor—which would have to be described as Apple White—glowed under the relentless light of dozens of fluorescent lights.

Richard Grant, the CEO, was waiting at reception.

"Thanks for meeting with us," began Boris.

"You're welcome, happy to help the law whenever possible."

"I'm Detective Sergeant Boris McDonald and Alice is helping us with this case. Speaking of which, can we come through?" He indicated the electronic turnstiles with a head tilt.

They were soon on the first floor in an open-plan office. Four lines of double-sided desks filled the room and at one end there were three or four glass-walled meeting rooms. The place was empty, so they grabbed seats from adjacent desks and spun them around.

"So, what can I help you with?" Richard started with.

"We found this card and were wondering what you could tell us about it?" Boris handed over the postcard which was in its own plastic evidence bag.

"Ah yes," began Richard, turning the card over in his hands, "we're aware that some of our welcome postcards got sent out by our marketing department, in error. We're aware of the GDPR implications and have actioned procedures that ensure they don't happen again."

Boris looked blankly at Alice, who leant over and whispered in his ear.

"New customers didn't give permission for marketing material to be sent to them. They sent the welcome postcard anyway. That's against the law and he's saying they've addressed the issue. The GDPR law protects against spam."

"Ah yes, thanks for that. But we're here about the party that the postcard was addressed to. We're following up some of the packages that they've sent."

Richard leant back in his chair and spread his hands.

"Ah, I'm afraid I can't help you there. We don't maintain a list of what we deliver."

Boris frowned. "So, you are shipping goods without knowing anything about what it is or who is shipping it?"

Richard looked defensive. "We allow people to utilise vacant shipping capability that would otherwise go unused. Which is a waste of carbon and greenhouse gases. We make the customer attest that they comply with the rules of the cartage company that will ultimately be used and included in that is a list of prohibited goods."

Boris wasn't satisfied with that explanation. "But they could be shipping anything?"

Richard tried a different tack. "Well, if you use FedEx or UPS or anyone, you can place anything in the parcel. Nobody X-rays all their parcels, it's not possible."

Boris decided to cut to the chase.

"OK, we're going to need to access your database."

Richard frowned back. "And I'm going to need to see a warrant."

Boris tried again. "We're following a lead which indicates that your network is being used to send materials which will be used in a terrorist attack—which could lead to the deaths of hundreds of people."

The realisation of the importance of the visit began to dawn on Richard, almost like a visible wave across his face.

"Ah, that's not good," he managed.

"So, you'll help?" persisted Boris.

Richard looked at him over steepled hands. "This is a very serious situation. Time is obviously of the essence, but I'm going to have to take advice from my legal counsel. Can you give me a minute?"

Boris was suspicious, but hopeful at the same time. "Sure."

Richard walked away with his phone to his ear. A few moments later he came back.

"OK, my lawyer is on the way. We're protected from liability under cartage statutes, but we have an obligation to the privacy of our customers. We can't just let the legal community have unfettered access to our data. So whatever warrant we get will have to be very specific in terms of the data that you're interested in."

"Our anti-terrorism laws give us a fairly wide set of powers. You do understand the time criticality of what we're talking about? You do understand that lives are on the line here?"

"Look I'd like to help you out but if my clients discover I turn over data to law enforcement when I don't have to, nobody will use my services ever again and my house is collateral for my business lending."

"How many people will want to use your services if it's discovered that you obstructed a police investigation and had the chance to stop the deaths of innocents?"

"Excuse me, officer, are you threatening my client?" Alice looked up. Two immaculately suited men strode purposely towards them.

"I'm Johan Bernier, and this is my colleague, Sam Wisden."

Boris shook their hands, introducing himself and Alice as a 'Technical Expert'. Boris then tried again. "Can we get your analytics guys down to find the shipments?"

Richard frowned apologetically. "I'm afraid they're actually all on an offsite."

Boris checked his watch. It was about six in the evening. "Well, can you get them back?"

Richard smiled. "They will not be of much use even if we did. They're a young team who work hard, play hard. I think they've probably knocked off for the day and will have had about two hours of drinking under their belts already."

"So how are we going to find the packages?" Boris was running out of patience. One step forward two steps back.

There was a period of behind-cupped-hands whispering between client and lawyers. Eventually, some sort of agreement was reached.

"Well, I guess we could allow supervised access to our database as long as the data does not leave the premises. We also want you to acknowledge that we have helped in your investigation, and as well as that, we have preserved the privacy of our clients. Now, as all our techs will have gone home, it'll take me a few hours to see if we can get any of them back into the office. And the offsite is out in the countryside, so it'll take some time to see if anyone is sober enough to come back." He got out his phone and started to scroll through his contacts list.

Alice spoke up. "I could have a look at it. I know databases. What tech stack are you using?"

Richard looked up, surprised. Recovering, he switched gears. "I don't know—I'll get our infrastructure guy on the line."

Alice frowned as Richard got up and paced while talking.

Boris noticed the frown and leaned closer. "What's wrong?" he asked.

"How many entrepreneurs do you know that don't know the intimate workings of their product? How does he not know the programs and languages his product is built with?"

"I don't know," responded Boris "—maybe he's more Steve Jobs rather than Steve Wozniak?"

Alice looked up sharply at the astute tech history reference.

Boris laughed, delighted at her response. "I'm not a Luddite just because I'm in the force," he chortled. "I read. I know things."

THE HUNT

An hour later Alice sat at a desk in an open-plan office consisting of a half dozen rows of clean white desks with four workstations each serviced by two monitors and all bathed under fluorescent lighting. All the monitors faced the same direction giving a vague sense of a classroom. Various coding books and tech detritus were the only other things of interest around. Outside, it had been raining, and the streetlights and shopfronts were reflected in the wet surface of the street as people hurried home from the pub, making Alice feel even more divorced from normal life.

The Infrastructure Manager arrived, shaking an umbrella in reception before passing through the turnstiles and introducing himself as Simon Brown. He was obviously pissed off—whether because of the rain or the lateness of the hour or both, Alice was unsure. He had a huddled conversation with the lawyer and Richard which did nothing to improve his mood and then returned to Alice and Boris.

"I can get you access to the database server, which should have everything you need."

"That's great, thanks" replied Alice, taking the Post-it note showing the log-in details for the workstation.

"Richard, Simon, is there any documentation? Any internal wiki or online shared knowledge base?"

Richard deferred to Simon who smiled fiendishly over from his chair. "Just what you can see there, unfortunately."

"Great, starting from scratch," she muttered under her breath.

She looked around the office, clearing her mind before leaping in.

The office disappeared as the screen filled her consciousness, focusing on learning what files were available, exploring the limits of her permissions and trying to piece together what programs were installed and what she'd need.

Two hours passed just like that.

She had found the team intranet and some documentation on the code for the website, which gave some clues to the structure of the database, but nothing on the actual data. She did find raw data files though.

She looked around the office again. Things had changed a little.

The lawyer had been replaced by a younger version. Not quite as well dressed. He looked a little like he was playing dress-up, his suit jacket half a size too big. He was awkwardly perched on an office chair at the end of the desk, texting on his phone, biting his lip in the blue glow.

Richard was playing something explosive on his phone. Thankfully the sound was off, and he was facing her so that the flashing colours played along the walls of the office behind him instead of distracting Alice.

Simon was dozing in his chair in the darkened corner of the office, the main lights only on over Alice's desk—like spotlights on a stage.

"No pressure", she thought bitterly. While she had all the information she needed, it wasn't in any sort of accessible format, so she woke Simon gently and asked again if there were any other servers or databases she would be able to get access to instead. Boris must have sensed her frustration and came over from his seat on the other side of the office.

"How's it going?" he asked, as she returned to her desk away from Simon.

"I can't find shit. Either they've given me access to the wrong server or the wrong database or both. Either way, nothing makes sense and I'll have to reconstruct the database from the files which *are* there." Alice's body language spoke of her opinion of that situation.

"So do you have what you need?"

"I would prefer to have the database in one piece so I can just do a search on it, but they've given me access to just the component parts. So they can say that they're helping us, but I will have to recreate the database, so it will take some time.

"I think so—it's just going to take a while to get the information out."

"Ah, so they've given you the ingredients and expect you to cook the meal yourself? OK. Coffee?"

"A tea would be awesome, thanks. Milk, no sugar."

Boris found his way to the coffee station and came back with an oversized mug with code emblazoned on the side. He assumed it was something incredibly clever and humorous.

Alice blinked and looked up. More time had passed—her tea had drunk itself.

"Fuck, what's the time? I'm starved."

Boris jumped to his feet. "I'll get some takeaway—any dietary requirements?" He nudged Simon awake. "Food run—what do you want?"

Thirty minutes later Alice was ploughing her way through a takeaway box of vegetable chow mein, one eye on the screen, one leg tucked under her and the other dangling over the arm of the expensive Aeron office chair. Her script was running its way through the files, the text on the screen slowly updating its slow progress. She turned her attention to Boris.

"So, level with me. Will you guys ever get around to Danica's case?"

Boris looked rueful. "Let me answer that this way. It's traumatic getting a picture of some guy's genitals, right?"

Alice agreed.

"But you know that police resources are limited. So, we have to make choices. And if you had to choose between investigating that or stopping some guy from beating up his wife. And if the worst that would happen to the dick pic guy would be a warning, you have to weigh up the cost/benefit calculation."

"Still sucks having that thrust in your face though."

Boris smirked at her use of language. Briefly.

Not wanting to let it go, Alice continued. "Why do guys send them?"

"Speaking on behalf of my gender?"

Alice nodded, smiling, and acknowledging the unfairness.

"Well, I don't know myself. I married young, so I didn't do the internet dating thing. When I was dating, you'd get set up by friends or dated within your wider circle of acquaintances, so even if you were a dickhead, you were beholden to people you cared about, so you didn't misbehave. And you only got set up with people who were serious about being in a relationship. Some of the younger guys in the station tell me about their experiences online. Strikes me that a lot of people on these apps don't actually want a relationship. Window shopping, ego boosting, I don't know. Dick pics though? Like a bird showing off its plumage? I guess it's a numbers game. If you only want one thing, then it's the minimal effort to see if you're going to get it. Take the one photo, send it to a million people. If you get a 1% of 1% response rate, that's still... a whole bunch of women who respond well to that sort of thing. Boom, you're in business."

Alice looked at him sharply.

"No, no, I'm not justifying it. Despicable. Ridiculous behaviour. But I also don't know how you get people to stop. Let's say we found some downtime between rape and murder cases and followed up on your friend's case. Seems easy, right? Look up the sender's phone number or email address. Chase him down, turn up at his place of work. Give him a stern talking to. He promises not to do it again. Justice done? Would your friend be happy with that? Make him apologise?"

"I guess there's a reason the victims of the crime aren't in charge of the punishments."

"Yeah... keeps the lawyers and judges in a job too."

A few minutes of silence passed. The letters and numbers on the screen continued ticking slowly through their workload.

"So, what's your story anyway? You mentioned you were looking for a job?"

"Yeah, I got back from Oz last week, so I'm looking for some coding contract work."

"Ah, Australia! Is the weather all it's cracked up to be?"

"Better. Sunshine, beaches, the whole thing."

"Where were you?"

"Sydney."

"Nice. Big city. So why did you come back?"

It was an innocent question, and while Alice had been expecting it, it still hit her harder than she expected.

"Things..." she managed "Things didn't turn out quite the way I expected."

"Oh?" He was just putting the ball back in her court.

"There was... an incident. Something happened at work."

Silence.

"I guess from the client's point of view, I didn't perform."

"And from your point of view?"

"Let's just say there were some undocumented expectations around some code that was written."

"How bad was it?" Boris joked. "Did someone get two pizzas instead of one?"

"A bit more serious than that." Alice's voice lowered. "Someone died."

Boris' face dropped. "Oh shit, I'm so sorry."

"Yeah, not my fault, but that sort of thing follows you around. Seemed like it would be easier to come home rather than try to fight the 'she said, he said'."

The screen blinked, and Alice straightened up in the chair.

"Hey, could you give me a few minutes? I need to concentrate on this for a bit."

"Of course!" Boris said, standing up. "Do you need anything?"

"Nah, I'm good. Thanks."

The green writing on the screen absorbed Alice entirely. The psychological state in which she was so focused on the code that the rest of the world dropped away was supposed to be called 'flow', and it was in that state that she was the most productive. But Alice called it her Wonderland. Not because of any connection to the Mad Hatter or the rabbit with the clock. No, it was where she could create wonder—like a sculptor making a statue by chipping away the parts of the marble which weren't part of the finished product in the artist's mind. Or, more accurately, like some sort of mental artificer making the components of a watch and then assembling them into a perfect miniature apparatus which could tell the time to an unbelievable level of accuracy. You could still achieve productivity by not entering the Wonderland, but the results were hard work and prone to bugs. When she was in the zone, the code flowed effortlessly and elegantly. Headphones and familiar music helped—anything which killed off distractions.

You'd think that a fatality due to her code would have come from not being able to enter Wonderland, but she'd been a victim of circumstance. Or so she told herself. The client had been a hospital and the software she'd been working on was an inventory system for items used in operations. Keeping tabs on every scalpel, swab and clamp used in every procedure. She'd been told that the database that would be storing the data was self-locking. So, when two commands came through at the same time, it was called a race condition. One command may have been 'give me all the materials attached to procedure number 1234' and another might be 'update that we've collected scalpel number 9876 in procedure 4567'. The two commands raced to see which would be executed first. A database that monitored and handled the race conditions didn't need any further code to decide which command went first or how to handle the errors which might occur. But if the database was less sophisticated, you would need additional code to see if a different command was reading or writing to the database before you could do your command. If one command tried to update all the items in a particular procedure while the other command tried to get a list of all the items in the same procedure, did the list include or exclude that update? A self-locking database would handle those race conditions. A non-self-locking database needed you to write that logic yourself.

The client had claimed she'd been negligent because it was lazy to rely on the built-in functionality to handle the race conditions. She had countered by saying that, since the technology was specified she should have been able to rely on it. She knew that the flavour of the database that they had used had been changed at the last minute for cost reasons and, with a fatality being the result, everyone was scampering to protect themselves. She suspected that the company that she worked for wouldn't back her and the court case would have been a constant reminder of that death. She had lost a lot of sleep around that time, waking screaming with the image of the person who had died firmly locked in her mind's eye.

On the plane flying back to the UK from Australia, she'd decided that she'd been cowardly for backing away from the fight. It would have been unpleasant, yes, but she should have had it out in court. She should have stood up for herself. She vowed that it would never happen again. She knew her stuff, why couldn't she just be left alone to do her job? Why did all this other stuff—other people's penny-pinching or political games or conflicts—have to get in the way of the job she was doing? She didn't particularly like the whole technology thing but, compared to the complexity of dealing with humans, it was easy.

And she'd never been to Wonderland while dealing with people. Only with code.

She'd rebuilt the SpareSpace database from scratch based on log files that were the only data on the server. Every change to every entity in the database was stored in these files, which was why they were so large. Then she had to collapse the data down to the most recent change, to see what the data looked like right now. Finally, after all of that, she had to figure out how the components fitted together. And that was before she even began to look for the deadly shipments.

But now it was starting to come together, and she had to figure out how to search for the shipments. Looking for a single shipment of a hundred packages wasted a fair bit of time as she discovered that shipments of that size were unlikely to be the cars. The parcel dimensions weren't listed, but the mass was, and the thought that the shippers might have lied about the weight of the package didn't occur to her until she was well through the list of shipments.

Google gave her an idea of the likely weight of the parcels—the brand of remote-controlled car was apparently 20lbs which turned out to be a little under 9kg in metric measurement, while the Skorpion, depending on what calibre and how many rounds it took, could be anywhere between 1.5 and 2kg, so she was looking for a parcel between 10.5 and 11kg.

After she'd ruled out all the single shipments of one hundred parcels, she started to go through the customers who had a total number of packages to be shipped of about one hundred, where each was above 10kg but below 15kg.

This brought up a lot of shipments leaving London and heading to the suburbs (toys and hardware goods going from shipping depots to shops) and animal feed and other supplies being sent out to farms. She almost missed the combination shipments from one farm out in Norfolk which stood out because it was coming back into the city. The address was for a pig farm but what would a pig farm be sending *into* the city in bulk which didn't require refrigeration? She almost fell off her chair when she discovered bulk loads being delivered to the farm in the last month: a hundred and ten RC controls from China and "farming equipment" from the Czech Republic. 'I wonder if a bulk order for a hundred cell phones with sim cards was making its way to the farm so that the pigs could post selfies to social media,' she wondered, and giggled tiredly to herself at the mental image.

SUCCESS

The sky was lightening when Alice looked up after finding what she'd spent all night searching for. The couch in reception had been taken over by the young lawyer, somehow able to supervise her use of company assets from thirty metres away through his eyelids. Richard had disappeared around 1am and Simon not long after that.

Boris had moved into one of the offices, napping under the desk on a pair of bean bags he'd found in a break-out room between the foosball table and fully-stocked drinks fridge. He'd checked in on Alice a few times in the early hours, but she'd been in a world of her own and he deemed it more beneficial to make a cup of tea and leave it within arm's reach. Whenever he came back it was empty, so he figured it was useful.

Alice had been comforted by the soft rumble of his distant snores—without her headphones, it was the next best thing in helping her to get in the zone. She finished jotting down the details on Post-it notes and nudged him awake.

"Got something for you," she said gently, beckoning to her workstation.

He followed her, bleary-eyed and stretching to get the kinks out.

"There we go," she said, pointing to the screen.

Boris scanned the gibberish. "Huh? What does it mean?"

"Oh, sorry. In plain English, this is what we've got—the parcels originated at a farm in Norfolk and were split into 4 equal shipments. All bound for London—Carnaby Street. Weirdly, one of them was misrouted through Milton Keynes—that one is still at the depot due to be delivered on Monday. Two of them are still at the depot in Norwich—no availability for Saturday delivery so they're also going to arrive on Monday".

"And the other one?"

"On its way now—due to be dropped off in the first run this morning and the delivery van is already on the road."

"Great work—do you have a delivery address?"

"They allow them to drop them off on the side of the road."

"So that's what they're going to do? Just drop them outside Carnaby Street? Then we have 25 radio-controlled cars with guns running amok on the busiest shopping street?"

"Yes."

"So how do we stop them?" Boris was already fumbling to get his phone out of his pocket.

"They're controlled from the website, yeah? But we haven't found where that is on the internet."

"So, we can't disable the website," agreed Boris.

"Or stop people from using it with a DDoS."

"Huh?" Boris responded, not the best this early in the morning.

"We can flood the website with traffic so it goes down. Like when too many people try to get concert tickets when they go on sale and the website can't cope with the load, so it goes down."

"Ah, ok—so if we can't block control by taking down the site, can we stop the website from accessing the cars?"

"If we could block the signal from getting to the cars, that would work."

"The wifi?"

"No, not wifi—the internet access will be from the cell phone network."

"Oh! So all we have to do is take down the cell coverage around that area, then that will stop anyone from controlling the cars." Boris was starting to get excited.

"Unless there's some backup plan for controlling the cars, then... yeah"

"OK, let's go. Do you have all the details of the truck with the cars?"

"Hang on, how are you going to block the cell phone signal?"

Boris was lost in thought or was ignoring the question—getting to his feet and getting out his cellphone.

"Do you have an Oyster?" he asked, referring to the public transport card.

"Yeah."

"C'mon, we can meet the guys at Piccadilly Circus on the way."

"Hang on, here are the addresses and consignment numbers for the other three shipments."

"Ah cool, thanks, let's go."

He helped her climb over the security gates, pausing to wake and thank a totally confused young lawyer before heading out into the street. The lawyer watched them blearily as they set off at a jog, Boris at first trying to type on his phone while running before giving up to focus on the journey.

The streets had quickly dried after the overnight rain and were filling with pedestrians on their way to work, street cleaners and the odd jogger. There were a few wisps of cloud picking up the red and gold of the dawn and a light breeze which should have reminded Boris of the last time he was out this early—when he ran the scene team outside Flannel earlier in the week. Instead, his mind was calculating a plan of action as he dodged tourists and families coming into the city for shopping expeditions. They kept to the left-hand side of the steps leading to the tube station, with Alice tucked in behind Boris. 99% of the pedestrian flow was going in the other direction which made them feel like salmon swimming against the flow of a river. As soon as they passed through the ticket barrier, Boris was on his phone, sending emails and texts based on the Post-it with the delivery details that Alice had given him.

Totally ignored by Boris, and jammed into a rush-hour train, all Alice could do was fret. She didn't know what Boris had in mind, but she did know that time was of the essence. She had done zero-sleep all-nighters at crunch time on a few contracts and they always backfired—the code which seemed good enough at the time was always replaced when the bugs the code generated were discovered in the cold light of day. She'd learned eventually to proactively manage the client so that the all-nighter was no longer an event that occurred—but last night was obviously an exception. She recognised the numbness—the disassociation—as if her body didn't belong to her and knew she wouldn't be making the best decisions. That wouldn't matter. Disabling the threat of the delivery was the only thing that mattered.

She kept an eye on Boris, who was leaning against the wall of the train, laser-focused on his phone the whole trip. When he roused, as they arrived at Piccadilly Circus, she manoeuvred through the crowd to follow him, apologising under her breath at the inevitable encroachment into other people's personal space, until they both popped out of the train onto the platform and then joined the flow of people heading out of the station. Boris turned and smiled with relief when he saw that she was right behind him. Together they surfed the swell of humanity as it forced its way to the ticket hall and then through the turnstiles and up the stairs to street level.

She followed Boris out and saw that he was talking to a policeman in a police car double-parked on the curb outside. She knew where she was, she knew where she had to go and so she set off at a sprint towards Carnaby Street, ignoring Boris' surprised yell after her. In her exhausted state it was like being on fast forward: overtaking the dawdling pedestrians, dodging traffic and then the child going flying. Leaving Regent Street and the back roads bordering Soho's seedier neighbourhood, so close to the upmarket shopping district and yet such a different flavour, always running, getting closer.

In the distance, the delivery truck appeared and she confronted the driver, getting nowhere with him until Boris turned up, drenched in sweat, puffing and blowing like a steam engine. The driver seemed to take comfort in the appearance of the police and looked vaguely bemused when the sirens coalesced into numerous police cars and vans which blocked the road around them. Someone who wasn't bemused was Boris, his face a deep red, the veins in his neck bulging.

"What were you doing? What would you have done if the packages had opened?" he managed between gasping breaths. "You could have been killed!"

Alice tried to manage her thoughts. She actually had no idea what she was trying to do—she had no idea how to disable the remote-controlled cars. She'd equated being first to the scene with being able to stop the expected carnage but, given a second of clarity, she admitted to herself that she'd put herself in danger with no upside. She was gutted that after all her good work on the investigation in the SpareSpace offices she had dropped the ball at the delivery point.

"You're lucky we're blocking the signal with Stingray," he continued after a few minutes of catching his breath, "you bloody idiot! What would you have done if they'd been active?"

What would she have done if she'd been faced with twenty-five remote-controlled cars each with a gun embedded in it? She felt sick. Boris read her face and realised that she got it. He placed his hands on her shoulders and looked carefully into her eyes. "Look, don't run off like that again. You damned near killed me. We have a special box which intercepts cell phone signals—Stingray. It means that the people who were trying to control the cars from their website couldn't take control of them. The bomb guys are going to take over in case there are secondary devices we have to worry about. Speaking of which..." he led her away from the delivery van towards the police cars which had blocked one end of the street. They stepped into one of the chain coffee shops and Boris grabbed a couple of cupcakes and cans of drink, paying by card. "Look, I've got a day's worth of policing to do here, how about you go home and get some sleep. We'll grab a coffee tomorrow and debrief, ok?"

She smiled tiredly and bit into her cupcake, before starting to make her way back towards the nearest tube station. Her muscles were starting to make twin complaints—up all night at a computer desk plus a headlong sprint without stretching, and she could feel a "lack of sleep" headache starting. "You did good, Alice!" yelled Boris as she trudged off.

THE AFTERMATH

Boris met Alice at a bike shop that doubled as a cafe near the Barbican. He was sitting in the far corner of the long narrow room, his back to the wall and a very frothy looking coffee in front of him, mounds of whipped cream obscuring the liquid beneath. You could almost split the interior of the cafe into three parts: a table with stools looking out of the floor-to-ceiling windows overlooking the street outside, pot plants and bicycles sporadically placed on top providing some form of privacy from outside scrutiny; in the middle of the room, a row of small square wooden tables and chairs provided seating for face-to-face conversation; while the rest of the space was taken up with the workshop and racks of accessories and bike parts.

There were a few other customers spotted around the interior, most perched at stools and focused on their laptops. Boris looked up as Alice entered. He looked terrible, which Alice attributed to the sleepless night but, as she got closer, she sensed there was something else going on. He smiled at her sadly as she sat herself down opposite him, waving at the girl behind the counter. The waitress came over wiping her hands on her apron as she did so.

"We don't actually have table service. If you'd like to come to the counter, I can take your order there," she said apologetically.

"Uh... ok," said Alice. "I'll be right over."

"Hey, how'd you sleep?" asked Boris.

"Yeah, good thanks. I needed it. What's the matter?"

Boris took a swig of coffee which was probably fifty percent cream, wiping the remnants which ended up on his face with a napkin before replying. "Just work stuff," he said. "I got hauled over the coals quite badly for including you in the investigation."

Alice was shocked. "But we stopped the cars! If we hadn't moved when we did, who knows who would have died?"

Boris wiped his eyes ruefully. "Yes. If the deaths had happened, I would have been asked if there was anything else I could have done. And saying 'nothing within the rules' wouldn't have brought any of the people back from the dead, would it? It boils down to this—if there are multiple deaths then that's a disaster, so it would've been ok to break the rules. But when there are no deaths because you were successful in preventing it, then all of a sudden there's great scrutiny. Great scrutiny," Boris said, trailing off. "I'm suspended for two weeks while there's an investigation. Speaking of which, after this coffee, you and I should probably not be in contact for those two weeks. I don't want anyone accusing me of trying to tamper with a witness."

"I am so sorry, Boris. I didn't realise you would get in trouble."

Again said with the sad smile. Alice's heart broke to see him looking so forlorn.

"Me too. You'd better get your coffee."

She went up to the counter, the blackboard on the wall showing pretty standard cafe fare, slightly more weighted toward the vegan and gluten-free, but all reasonably priced. She was behind a couple who were checking the ingredients of half the menu to ensure they were all locally sourced. As she waited, she heard Boris's cell phone go off and be answered. When it was her turn at the counter, she ordered a cappuccino, paid for it, and returned to the table just in time to see Boris hang up.

"Are you busy today, Alice?" he asked. "I've just got off the phone with someone from the Home Office who wants to talk to us."

She frowned as she sat down. "On a Sunday?"

Boris nodded. "I'm pretty sure the Independent Office for Police Conduct only work Monday to Friday, so I don't think it's them."

"Which part of the Home Office?"

"They didn't say. Mike Reid is the guy's name. Said he could be here in an hour. I'll try and see if they can pay for our lunch. Might as well get something out of a pre-firing roasting."

"So how does the Home Office become involved with the Police?"

"Well, the Home Office is a governmental agency—they handle border security, most of the police and the IOPC. They're the ones who will be asking a lot of questions. And then, if they think I've gone too far, they'll refer the case to the CPS —Crown Prosecution Service. And if they agree, then... well, I might be in the market for a lawyer."

"That sucks. This whole thing sucks."

"I think the Force might be feeling a little embarrassed by the perceived need to go outside for IT resource. Our tech guys are brilliant, but there are way too many cases for them to be everywhere. And that will be the obvious angle of the story, right. And you know the press will be looking to break the story. I'm surprised that you haven't been door stopped yet. That's when the press turn up, knock on your door and take your photo before you realise that they are there. Usually followed by a swarm of them standing outside your house with their long lenses and yelled questions. Fun time."

"Wow, quite something to look forward to, huh?"

There was a moment of silence, as they came to the terms of their probable immediate future. Then Boris took another gulp of coffee, not bothering to wipe the cream off the end of his nose and turning to Alice with a manic grin. She laughed at the white clown nose and the sombre mood lifted. "We did good, Alice. No matter what happens, I want you to know that we did the right thing. We did save those shoppers. I probably could have done without the sprinting, but we did good. You've got a knack."

Alice changed the subject, unused to such gushing praise and they filled the hour that they were waiting by chatting about Boris's wife and Alice's cousin Zoltan. There was a steady stream of people bringing their bikes in to be looked at by the workshop, some svelte and fit, some less so. Boris looked up at one point and commented.

"I haven't seen so many *mamils* in a long time."

Alice looked around and frowned. "Mammals?"

Boris smiled at her taking his bait. "*Mamils*—'middle aged men in lycra'. But, man, they're taking their lives in their hands in London!"

"Apparently it's a great way to get fit," allowed Alice, noticing, as she said it, a new customer enter the cafe. He was about average height, black, quite good-looking, and dressed very well in a T-shirt that showed off his well-muscled physique. Not bulky, like a wrestler—more chiselled. He had a blazer on over the T-shirt and finished the ensemble with a chunky pair of camel-coloured thick-soled boots. He spotted her looking and smiled disarmingly. She felt herself colouring and turned back to Boris. He was smiling at her as well.

"We could ask if he has any lycra," he teased.

"Boris? Alice?" They looked up and there he was, still smiling at her, somehow having gotten served immediately and making his way to their little corner of the store in the blink of an eye.

Boris stood up uncertainly and shook his hand, and then the newcomer turned to Alice and shook hers too. His handshake was gentle yet firm, as he emphatically stated his name. "Mike Reid. Thanks for waiting for me, I really appreciate it."

Boris sat back down. "You're welcome, though it is getting close to lunchtime..."

Mike smiled at them both again as he sat down at the single chair opposite them and took off his blazer, hanging it on the back of his chair. He had the air of someone meeting up with old friends that he hadn't seen for a while. All bonhomie and friendliness. Boris and Alice shared a glance. Not what they were expecting at all. "Well, let's see how our chat goes and maybe we can persuade the purse holders that the government should buy our lunch."

Boris had a puzzled look on his face. "You mentioned that you worked for the Home Office and I was trying to figure out which part—are you part of the IOPC? CPS?"

"So suspicious Boris! What are you hiding?" Mike responded chidingly.

"I just wanted to know whether I should have brought my lawyer," Boris said evenly.

"Oh! Sorry, no, I should have realised. No, I'm not part of any of that. Sorry, I should have said—no, I didn't mean to worry you. You're right, the Home Office has a large portfolio of responsibilities, it's only natural to wonder where I fit in. I've been working on an inter-departmental intelligence commission since the Insurrection back in 2020, so part of the Home Office, but not actually in any of the departments. But interacting with all of them. And I've got some contacts in certain teams within the Force who let me know when certain events of interest, or certain characters of interest pop up."

A silence filled their section of the cafe as Boris and Alice digested what Mike had told them. "Ok, I'll bite," said Alice at last. "Who has triggered your interest?" She was mentally going through the list of all her friends who had helped her, hoping that none of them was a suspect in something bigger. The last thing she was ready for was for someone like Morocco Mike being in trouble for some immigration problem, or Fabian getting stung with something unsavoury involving porn.

"We actually still don't know his real name. I've been calling him The Handler, but he has gone by a number of aliases."

"I don't understand—who would we know him as?"

"Oh, I don't think that you've met him. But he's been in the background and we—or at least I—think that we might be able to work together to finally get him."

Boris blinked twice, before leaning back in his seat. "Sounds like quite the tale. Maybe one to share over a burger? I've had my eye on the fried chicken burger here for a while."

Mike nodded, getting up from his seat and collecting his blazer. "And for the lady?" he asked over his shoulder.

The tables had the menu on them, printed on A5 paper, the font a little small for Alice's liking if she was honest. There were plenty of vegetarian options and, as she quickly read them, she realised that she was quite hungry. "I'll have the mushroom burger please," she said.

Mike headed to the counter, and Boris leaned forward, suddenly intense. "What do you think?"

Alice smiled uncertainly. "I think we'll get a meal and answer some questions and then I can go back to trying to find a job while you get to do some gardening for two weeks."

Boris shook his head and looked thoughtful. Once Mike had returned, Boris cleared his throat. "Hey, Mike, just in case I have to run, can I get a business card? Just so that I've got your number."

Mike dug awkwardly behind himself trying to find the inside breast pocket of his blazer which he had already put on the back of the chair before standing up and taking it off the chair and getting out his wallet. "Of course, very wise," he said, handing one to Alice as well. "It's got the office number as well, but that just goes to voicemail. I don't have much of a staff unfortunately. But it's all legit."

Alice turned the card over in her hand. Matt stock, official looking logo, an address which might or might not be real, Mike's name. Nothing to raise alarm bells, but nothing different than what you could get at any printer. She eventually put it in her own wallet.

Mike considered them each, watching as they stared at the business cards he'd just handed over. "Not exactly the most compelling of bona fides, right? Anyone could print out a hundred of these for a fiver. If you wanted to wait until tomorrow, I can make a few calls and get my boss to talk to your boss to vouch for me, but the other thing we could do is do a Google search for my name and 'BAME Home Office'."

Boris pulled out his phone and punched in the search, having to correct the spelling of Mike's surname, but bringing up a website with photos of various black, Asian and Middle Eastern employees of the Home Office. Looking a little embarrassed, Mike pointed at the link to the "Up and Coming" section. There they could see a photo of Mike accepting some sort of award, the background festooned with Home Office banners. Alice and Boris laughed and Mike rolled his eyes but it was enough, Alice noting the website had a gov.uk address which was proof enough for her.

"Whose is the chicken?" asked the waitress who had appeared out of nowhere.

"Ah, that's for me," said Boris, reaching for the burger which was surrounded by fries.

"And two mushroom burgers," she continued, placing them in front of Alice and Mike.

As she left and they started squirting condiments on the fries, Mike continued the conversation.

"OK, so we've collected a number of identities that we suspect The Handler has assumed over the last three years, though chances are good that they're not all him. They're all individuals with strong connections to Russian organised crime operating in this country and far enough removed to not be caught up in any actual police operations."

Boris frowned. "Have you got an example? I can't see how you would not be able to find him if he keeps popping up in your investigations."

Mike looked surprised, before nodding in agreement. "Yes, fair enough. Uhh... OK, there was a case where great quantities of cigarettes were being smuggled into the country."

It was Alice's turn to frown. "I'm sorry, cigarettes?"

Mike leaned back. "A twenty pack of cigarettes goes for £10. So a thousand costs £500. About half of that is duty and VAT. You can fit almost ten million cigarettes in a shipping container. So, if you only looked at lost revenue for Her Majesty's Customs, you're looking at over £2,000,000 per container. But it gets better than that. If you buy a shipping container's worth of cigarettes in Ukraine, you can pick them up for £150,000. If you sold them for half the retail price here in the UK, you could collect over £2,500,000, most of which is profit. So, very lucrative, right?"

Alice's eyes widened. "Wow."

"We tracked down someone who had set themselves up as an import/exporter to bring the containers in, with some local gang as the distribution network. The local constabulary rolled them up on some low-level drug operation. We followed the trail back through the local ports and followed up on what we found on the import manifests. The company details were a dead-end as you would expect, but the bank shared the documentation that the people opening the accounts had used. Passports were fresh and clean—we made some inquiries with our connections in Russia and found that the passports were new, as were the names used. As in, they didn't exist the year before."

Boris and Alice exchanged confused looks.

"Oh, sorry. It's like this. getting data from Russia is such an industry that people are taking copies of common databases all the time and putting them online. So that means that you can see suspicious activity popping up all the time."

Boris shook his head. "Nope, sorry, still don't follow."

Mike tried again. "OK, let's use you as an example. Your records appear in the database of births and deaths, right? There's a record of you being born on a particular day, in a particular hospital. And that record would have been logged within a couple of days of the birth. So, if I bought a copy of the births and deaths database last year, I would expect to see your name and date of birth in there. And, likewise, if I bought a copy of the database today I would expect to see your name and date of birth in there as well. But let's say I bought those two copies and in one of them, today's version, you appear in there. But in the older one you don't exist. What would that tell me?"

"It could mean that the registration of my birth got mucked up?" tried Boris.

"That's possible, yes. But you're what, thirty? Forty? The chances of them finding the paperwork and realising it didn't make it onto the database in the last year when it could have come to light at any time in the last thirty or forty years are pretty unlikely, right? Also, if you then look at the passport records and you see that someone with an import/export business didn't have a passport at all, just months before applying for bank accounts and import licenses, sounds a little suspicious. No international travel at all, and then boom, they're an importer/exporter? All possible, but..."—he grimaced in disbelief.

"So, you think that your man is... The Handler, did you call him?"

"Yeah, so we're pretty sure that The Handler was the guy on the Russian end."

"I thought you said the cigarettes were Ukrainian?"

"Funny story—the cigarettes were Ukrainian, but they were transhipped through Russia. We never found out if they were paying the local duty or just paying off the local customs agents. Anyways, although the passport used in the UK for the bank account was definitely not The Handler, we traced the other name—the guy handling the Russian end of the operation—on the company formation documents back to Russia and found the brand-new person records when there was a mistake with the data we bought. They gave us old data, we wanted new data, they corrected the issue, we compared the two datasets and found a whole lot of suspicious identities including our friend in Russia, who looked in his photos a lot like our friend The Handler. Over the course of the last eighteen months, this happens a fair bit with various crimes and various schemes. We occasionally pick up the local representative, usually as part of a police investigation, whether we give the intel to the local police or they tip us off and we add it to our accumulating pile of evidence, either way we're keeping tabs on him. And, of course, the guys we pick up don't tell us anything, but we look for anything connecting them, anything which gets us closer to our man—who definitely doesn't come to the UK, right? We know what he looks like."

Mike momentarily slowed, looking into the middle distance as if revisiting a piece of personal history, before snapping back to the now. "But his tendrils extend across from Russia to the UK."

"You mentioned that he was somehow connected to someone relating to the remote-control cars?"

"The team that ran the software development company that did the software for the cars turns out to be quasi legit. A lot of various clients, some with very specific requirements, and some generic ones looking for very basic automation or a website, that sort of thing. So as usual we look into the ownership structure of the business, and we come across some people who had been one of the owners four years ago but had sold their shareholding to the current owners. Nothing suspicious about that at all, right? We don't know when this software company started doing work for criminals, could have been before they sold out, might have been afterwards. But the name of the person who sold their shares then turns up in a leak of people transacting through the Bahamas."

Alice looked confused. Boris leaned over and said, "Tax haven, great for company secrecy—no way to track ownership."

Mike nodded. "Again, nothing out of the ordinary there, right? Except not long after they sell their shares in the software company, they invest in another company. A much more famous company. The holding company which owns all the businesses that Richard Grant runs."

Alice and Boris looked at each other. "So... The Handler is Richard Grant?" asked Alice.

"No... no," corrected Boris. "But he knows who he is. And if he needs to talk to him in person there's a good chance it will be in the UK. Or maybe Richard goes to Russia. Either way Richard is the connection."

Mike smiled and nodded, but he wasn't looking at Boris. He kept his eyes on Alice.

"Well, good luck with that. I imagine you'll be following Richard, maybe bugging his phone."

"Yes, they could do that, Alice, that's true. But I imagine that they would much rather have a person on the inside. Someone that could get close to Richard. Someone that they could trust," Boris said.

"Someone like you that has two weeks off coming up?"

Boris shook his head. "More like someone who has tech skills and who needs a job."

It took Alice a few minutes to figure out who he was talking about. And when she did, she shook her head violently. "No, no, no. Look, that's not going to work for so many reasons. Umm, first of all, are they hiring? Then what tech stack are they using? They're probably using languages that I don't know, or some bullshit framework that nobody else uses. And then even if they do have a job and it's for a skill that I have and that I somehow persuade them that I am right for the job, you *have* noticed that I'm a woman, right? And we're still not quite at the point in history that the best person for the job gets the job, and we don't know that I am the right person for the job, but let's say that I am and nobody else went to school with the hiring manager or that the hiring manager recognises that I am the right person for the job and isn't some misogynist," she paused for a breath, "even then, how the hell am I going to be able to 'keep tabs' on him? How many software developers do you know that keep tabs on the CEO's whereabouts?"

Mike finished his last French fry, chasing the last squidge of mayonnaise around his plate as he did so. "I believe that you will figure it out," was all he would say. "Give it some thought. I'll give you a ring on Monday first thing to see if you're keen. I'll have to have a chat with our friends over at Box. Wouldn't want them thinking that I was treading on their toes. Playing in their sandpit. Got to keep the peace." And with that, he bade them farewell. Just before he left, his blazer over one arm, he paused, cocked his head and said quietly to Alice, "I wouldn't ask you to do this if I didn't think you could do it. You did really well with the cars. Chat Monday." And then he was out the door.

Boris waited until he was sure that Mike had gone and then let out a low whistle. "You just got recruited! How do you feel?"

Alice sat, not quite numb, but still spaced out. "Give me a minute," she managed. She concentrated on her breathing. Focusing on slowing down and deepening her breaths. "Wow," she said. "So... what does being a secret agent pay?"

Boris smiled broadly. "The gratitude of the nation, I should think. I think that lunch will be the only thing you get out of our friend Mike."

Alice frowned. "Really?"

Boris shrugged. "Sometimes we pay our CIs, but I don't know if the Home Office does. Let's just say if you do get a job with Richard, make sure you get a good salary."

"What if that means I don't get the job?"

"But if you sell yourself as an awesome coder, then they will be suspicious if they can get you for a pittance, right?"

"I guess... You sound like you think that I will agree to do this for Mike."

"I think you've already decided to do it."

"And what do you think?"

"You get a job, they get intelligence. Sounds like a win-win. Just don't do anything that puts you in any danger. And keep my number in your phone..." Then, remembering his earlier admonishment, he amended his last comment. "Just don't get in any trouble where you need my help in the next two weeks, right?"

GETTING THE JOB

After her meeting with Mike and Boris on the Sunday, she'd gone home and chatted briefly with Zoltan. His plans for the rest of the Sunday revolved around gardening in the window box on the balcony in the flat, so she took her laptop and headed to the library. The Barbican complex included an Art centre, theatre, cinemas, as well as a library—all the result of planning conditions placed on the redevelopment of the site after being bombed to a husk in World War Two.

She needed the time to sit and think and the calm and quiet of the library was the perfect setting for weighing the pros and cons of taking a slight diversion in her career journey. She emerged a couple of hours later with the justification for the decision she'd pretty much made from the first time that Mike had mentioned his plan. She would, of course, do it. She told herself it was because she had nothing else to do and, worst case, it was a job, but in reality it was for two wholly different reasons. Number one, being connected to a millionaire entrepreneur would involve her in a social circle she'd never been in before and number two being the opportunity to follow the path further upstream and hopefully find the people involved with the remote cars. A 'justice boner' Danica described it—the visceral desire for justice. Alice had always wondered if that was misnaming the desire for vengeance, especially with Danica. But now she felt the rage within her at the wrong-doing that needed rectifying, she knew what Danica had been referring to.

The conversation on the Monday with Mike was short and to the point. He said that she should ring Richard Grant directly and ask for a job. No need for lying—she did need a job, and she was a perfect candidate for a role in a startup tech company. With the credentials to prove it. As long as they didn't check what happened in Australia, of course.

Mike dug out Richard's phone number and passed it on to Alice, and she didn't think to ask if he had it already or he had gotten it off Boris. Either way, she didn't hesitate to call him and lay out her case for employment. With their interactions so fresh in his mind he knew exactly who she was and the context in which he knew her. He had thought about it for maybe two minutes before agreeing that he would get her in for an interview and telling her to expect a call from the HR manager at SpareSpace before the day was out.

True to his word, she then had a five-minute conversation with Yamini from HR at SpareSpace which basically entailed checking that she was a British citizen and that she could make it for 3pm on Friday. As she hung up from the call she compared the recent weeks of emails, applications and stressful interviews which had gone nowhere with the simplicity of a single five-minute phone call with the right person. She definitely wanted to mix in these circles!

She still applied for other jobs during the week leading up to the interview but, to tell the truth, her heart wasn't really in it. Her focus was purely on the SpareSpace interview and she didn't want to jinx it by accidentally getting a different job in the meantime. She knew she should have done some research on SpareSpace, so that she could ask insightful, engaging questions that showed she wanted to work there. But her experience over the last week had given her some pretty rare insights into their business, the shortcomings of the business model as well as their technical platforms, so she wasn't quite sure what else would impress them. What year they were incorporated, or their company structure and shareholdings?

She didn't feel that she was being arrogant, merely that she was well prepared. Which is why the initial questioning had thrown her so much.

There were two of them in the interview. Alice always wondered if that was to avoid claims of some form of inappropriate behaviour from the interviewers, or if it was actually to get two opinions of the candidate like the HR folk always claimed. She was unsuccessfully trying not to call them Tweedledum and Tweedledee in her mind, but they were two well-meaning but wholly unsuitable interviewers. Tweedledum seemed to think that a collection of brain teasers would suffice, insofar as finding out if she was a good candidate was concerned, while Tweedledee was very big on Computer Science questions. For someone who learned by doing, it was a little frustrating. She could feel the interview slipping from her grasp. It was Tweedledum's turn to ask a question.

"How would you work out how many ping pong balls would fit in a 747?" he asked, then leaned back with a smirk.

She paused before asking him a clarifying question of her own. "Does the job require that sort of calculation a lot?"

"Like I said about the other questions, they may not sound as if they are pertinent to the job but they do show us how you think, and your thought processes are very important in regards to the role."

Alice finally figured that his smirk was supposed to be an encouraging smile. Chalk that one up to a lack of self-awareness.

"Fine. I'd measure the diameter of the fuselage, and the length of the plane. Work out the volume of the plane. Measure the volume of the ping pong ball, divide one by the other, and apply some sort of factor based on the fact that when you stack spheres there's wasted space between them."

"And what about the wings? The tail? The cockpit?"

"Sure, I'd measure them and estimate the volume within each part. Add them to the fuselage and apply the same factor."

He made some notes in his notebook.

Tweedledee leaned back in his chair and put his hands behind his head. "I wanted to make sure that you had enough time to ask any questions that you might have, so...?"

Alice thought back to her sleepless night in the same office she sat in now. A grin—almost evil in nature—flickered momentarily across her face. "I'm glad you asked that, I do have one or two. What kind of database do you use in production?"

Tweedledee blinked. "We use Hadoop," he said.

Alice nodded as if he'd said the sky was blue. "Yes, but do you have anything more performant? Anything quicker for analytics or reporting? Hadoop is great—it can take whatever data volumes you throw at it, but it's slow."

Tweedledee harrumphed. "It's free," he tried.

"So is Postgres," said Alice. "And what's with the partitioning you guys use? If you partition on sub day increments, it's going to make any queries run slow—most of your queries are going to take the whole day."

Tweedledum piped up. "If we partitioned on the day then the files would get too big. How do you know about our partitioning?"

"I recreated your database based off the backup files in less than six hours, re-indexed it so that it didn't perform like a dog when I ran my search queries and then found a needle in the haystack in less than another three hours. All on no sleep."

This met with a silence so profound, Alice was convinced she'd killed them. They sat there, eyes and mouths equally round and vacant, six ovals staring back at her.

"Bullshit," Tweedledee finally managed.

"Ask Simon. He's your infrastructure manager, right? He was there."

They looked at each other. The tone in the room changed. The smirks had gone. Tweedledee got up and fished a phone out of his pocket. "I can ring Simon and get him in here in two minutes," he said threateningly.

"I'd really like you to do that," she said fearlessly.

He finished dialling and tersely asked if Simon could join them.

As soon as Simon entered the room and saw Alice, he was on edge.

"What is she doing here?" he asked.

"Alice was just telling us that she recreated our database off the raw files in six hours. Did that really happen?"

"Yes, she had to do some work and the analytics team was on that offsite, so Richard got her access and she got what she needed overnight. Was there anything else you two needed?"

"Uh, no, thanks for that." Simon left.

"So that's question one. Question two is what languages and frameworks do you use?"

The rest of the interview was in stark contrast with the beginning. Alice teased out of them the details of the hodge-podge of technologies that they used. She even made them talk about some of the logic behind those decisions, discovering as she did so some of the political camps within the business. The revelation that she knew the CEO, the infrastructure manager and had gotten her hands dirty with their systems really put them on the back foot, and they somewhat apologetically revealed some of the challenges that they faced and the environment that they had created.

"So you can see that, while we would have liked an integrated release system, we really don't have the time to set up the infrastructure to allow that. And management deciding not to go to a cloud environment has really prevented us from using the latest technology."

"Hey, you're still a startup, it's never going to be everything you want it to be. I'm guessing the managers are all about speed to market—'just get this feature out now, we can worry about productionalising it later'—am I right?"

They were almost comically thankful that she got it. "And we tell them that if we don't spend the time to get it right then it will all fall apart, but they don't care—they're not the ones who have to come in on the weekend to fix it up when the pipelines go awry, right?"

"I know some tricks to try and fix that," she told them. Their eyes lit up.

"Like what?" they asked, not quite at the same time.

"That, gentlemen, you will find out in the first month. If I get the job of course. Last question—how many others are you interviewing for this role?"

They looked at each other. Tweedledee was the first to answer. "Well, we don't normally do interviews."

No shit, thought Alice.

"But we were told to put you through your paces, and I think that you know your stuff, so we'll feed that back to our HR people, and they'll take it from there. I didn't actually know we were hiring to tell you the truth."

"That's awesome, thanks for your time, and I'll look forward to working with you if I'm successful," Alice said as she shook their hands and headed for the door. They walked her to the security desk and waited while she signed out and handed back her visitor's badge before waving and heading back inside. Alice walked out to a slightly cloudy Friday afternoon in Holborn and started walking back towards the Barbican, considering how it had been a little too easy to get the job interview in the end. She was annoyed at how the two interviewers were using the interview as an ego-inflating exercise. The brain teaser guy was impressed with himself that he knew the answers to the brain teasers and while the supposed reason for asking them was to explore her reasoning abilities, the sort of reasoning and guesstimating that it tested for was nothing like the coding work she was imagining the role would entail. Likewise, the guy testing for Computer Science 101 concepts was showing off that he took courses at university, rather than focusing on the application of those concepts to coding problems. She idly wondered if they would have asked the same questions of a male applicant. And then she wondered which answer to that question would be worse.

On the walk home from the interview she texted Mike to let him know that she thought it had gone well, and that she'd let him know when she heard back from the SpareSpace people. And then she popped into the local

Waitrose on the way home to pick up a bottle of wine and the ingredients for a nut roast for dinner.

The weekend limped along. Alice tried to distract herself the best she could, but she had one eye on the phone the whole time, knowing full well that no decision was likely to happen over the weekend, and that it was more likely she would get some feedback mid to late the following week.

In fact, it was on Tuesday that she got a phone call from Yamini from HR at SpareSpace with the offer. She was in the lounge chatting with Zoltan and he watched her side of the conversation with interest. Alice had forgotten to research the going rate for permanent jobs in her area, so when Yamini mentioned the offer she was silent, not sure that she had heard correctly. Yamini interpreted the silence as disapproval and rung off, promising to get back to her with a higher offer in a few minutes.

Zoltan raised an eyebrow at the swiftness of the call and Alice's lack of contribution and when she told him the amount of the offer, he seemed perplexed at her response.

"I'm used to Australian dollars which are worth half as much—plus I'm used to contract rates. I guess it wasn't a bad offer really, but it's been so long since I've had a perm job, I'm quite unused to what makes a good salary."

"How much were you on in Australia?" asked Zoltan.

She told him and he whistled. "That's good going, would you be able to get something similar over here?"

She shook her head. "No, you see there's a premium that people pay contractors in exchange for being able to get rid of them as soon as they have finished the piece of work that they want you to do. I forgot about that, so when she said the salary, I should have said, 'That's lovely, thank you very much'."

Zoltan made a face. "Eeep! Do you think she'll be able to get you more? You haven't shot yourself in the foot, have you?"

"I hope not," she replied as her phone rang. She answered it quickly.

"Hello?"

Zoltan studied her face as the conversation proceeded, trying to establish what was being said from the micro reactions flitting across Alice's face. The short conversation ended when Alice said, "That would be lovely, thank you. Please send the papers over and I'll print them and sign them and put them in the mail."

Zoltan waited until she put the phone down before cocking his eyebrow. "...Well?"

She smiled and then grimaced. "They've given me another five thousand. I start next week."

Zoltan went straight into the kitchen and got a bottle of champagne from the fridge. "Break out the Bolly, baby!" he exclaimed as he began to peel the foil from the neck. "Well done, Alice! I must try to use that in my next negotiation - just ignore them when they tell me the salary on offer."

STARTING THE JOB

The first day came around quickly, and Alice was strangely excited by her new job. She had originally been in two minds about continuing a career as a coder but doing the undercover work for Mike had made it more palatable. She wondered idly if her return to permanent employment would take any period of adjustment—the adjustment to the salary had already taken some getting used to, though the trade-off of getting pension contributions, sick leave and annual holidays took some of the sting out of the difference in take-home pay.

She'd been told to ask for her manager when she arrived at reception and Oliver turned out to be a shortish middle-aged Spanish man with long straggly hair. He impishly welcomed her and showed her to her spot on the open-plan desk. Waiting for her was a brand-new laptop and external monitor.

"If you need extra monitors, just let me know," he said in heavily accented English. "Some people like having two, side by side, and if you really want to we can get four, but with four you get too much real estate and it can be hard to focus with so much area."

Alice nodded sagely. They walked over to Security, where Alice's photo was taken and a pass issued. Once she had the lanyard with the thick plastic picture on it, Oliver gave her a remote token that would allow her to access the office network from anywhere there was an internet connection. Oliver was just starting to go through the sign-on routine when Alice stopped him.

"Is there a notebook or something which I can write things on?" she asked. "There's a lot to take in."

Oliver slapped his forehead. "Sorry," he said, pulling out a cardboard wallet from under the laptop. "Here is your documentation, your employee contract, handbook, a notebook for you to take notes, a discount booklet with all the deals you get from all Richard Grant's companies and..." he trailed off as he ran out of things he could remember were in the pack. "Everything you might need," he finished off.

He walked her around the office, showing her where the toilets were, where the kitchenette was and where the smokers went for their nicotine fix. "Before lunch, we'll introduce you to the team and then we'll head out to the local pub so you can see the team in a less formal atmosphere."

Alice was a little bemused by the support being given to her on her first day—she was used to being given a computer and a desk and told to get to it. She was quite adept at getting up to speed on a diverse set of systems and code bases very quickly. It was the only way to be productive and therefore the only way for her to show value—essential for a contractor, especially with clients who didn't care that delays in delivery of code may be because of internal teams not getting around to providing permissions or log in details.

Because of her background, she hadn't expected to be introduced to the wider team and was, therefore, a little overwhelmed by the number of faces and names—there was no way she'd be able to remember them all. The ones that stood out were Oliver's and Cathy's.

Cathy was a short, mixed-race girl with long dark hair, shaved at the sides—about Alice's age or maybe a year or two older. She wore a black T-shirt, which barely covered tattoos on her upper arms, and black jeans. Nose studs, multiple ear piercings and a smattering of further tattoos on her hands told the world to keep back, but she was nothing but helpful to Alice, and they briefly chatted about some of their respective preferences for coding setups, while Oliver stood nearby, smiling encouragingly. Alice made a mental note to ask Cathy about that later.

After a whir of names and a blur of faces, they all headed out to the local pub. The others seemed to treat this as a bit of a jolly, with tomfoolery and jokes bouncing around the team as they made the short trip across the road and down a side street. While the pub had an outdoor area, they made their way inside to a private dining room where the dark wood panelling and atmospheric low lighting made seeing harder than it needed to be. Alice found herself sitting beside Cathy and, after they'd ordered their meals and a drink, Alice turned to her and asked about Oliver and the smiling.

Cathy grinned. "I know, weird right? It's happened in a few places I've worked. As near as I can figure it, female coders are still a novelty enough for some managers to have a strange amount of emotional investment in them getting along with each other. I used to think it meant that it was some sort of seal of approval that if the workplace was good enough for one woman to code there then the management wanted to make sure that you got that straight from the horse's mouth so to speak. But I don't know if it's that cerebral, really."

Alice was intrigued. "What else can it be?"

Cathay shrugged. "Fucked if I know—I just know if you want to mess with them, you just have to suggest that there is some sort of simmering undercurrent of conflict and watch them fall all over themselves trying to solve it."

Alice glanced up to see Oliver nodding approvingly at her and Cathy chatting, and shared a laugh with Cathy when she too noticed.

When the food came, the burgers were served on metal plates and the fries in little beaten copper cups. Alice was glad when her lager came in a normal beer glass, especially after seeing soft drinks being served in glass jars and festooned with mint leaves. Her colleagues seemed a good bunch. Young, which still tended to be the rule with start-ups in her experience. The banter was good-hearted, and while there were a few who stayed on the fringes of the jokes, by and large she was getting a friendly vibe. Oliver got the bill at the end of the lunch and the walk back to the office seemed a bit longer with a belly full of very greasy burger and fries, and all Alice really wanted to do was find a corner of the office, preferably out of the relentless light of the fluorescent lamps for a little nap.

The afternoon was taken up with familiarising herself with the systems and platforms that the team used for creating and releasing code, and by and large it all made sense. Basically, there was a system of cards with the details of what was required, and the coders would grab the next one off the pile and then work their way through creating the functionality. After testing it and integrating it with the rest of the code and checking that it hadn't broken anything else, it would be signed off and the card would be marked as completed. Very much like everywhere else that she'd worked.

After the familiarisation with the systems, there were some online training and videos to sit through which explained the company objectives, and Alice was all done by 4pm. Oliver checked in with her and they decided it was best for her to go home and to come in the next day ready to go. She thanked him for all his help and walked home.

When Zoltan asked how it had gone, she shrugged and said that she didn't know. Everyone was friendly enough and having logins and the correct permissions on day one was almost unheard of, but she'd learned the hard way that sometimes an awesome environment was ruined political games, and vice versa—she'd worked at one place where everyone had been super friendly and genuine, but they had no systems, no processes. As a result of that, everything was chaos. Nobody lasted long there, and she'd barely seen out the end of her contract.

The next day she went in early and started work on one of the cards. She selected the one from the top of the queue and got to work, only needing a few questions answered and she knew who could help her. The testing of her functionality went well and by lunchtime she was integrating her code into the main codebase.

That was a pattern that repeated itself during the week. She'd power through the tasks given to her and by and large everyone was happy with her production. The team started to notice how good she was, and everybody remained helpful and encouraging. She knew she had to prove herself for the sake of the job as well as any potential spying she may need to do, and so she focused all her energies into making sure she was producing good code and being a team player, which meant quietly achieving all this and making documentation so that anyone else having to support her code would be able to figure out what she was doing and how.

What she couldn't figure out is how they were making enough money to keep the lights on. There were a lot of coders, infrastructure managers, testers and analytics people, and if they were all on similar money to what she was on, then they would have to be bringing in a lot in sales or subscription income. But Alice couldn't see how the customer base she was aware of would be able to bring in enough income from using other people's unused logistics capacity. Having full access to the data behind the business meant that she could see the transactions in real-time and could monitor the income which followed them. If this was all the money they were making, then they were truly haemorrhaging cash. She tried to bring this up with Oliver at one of their debriefing sessions.

"So, if that's all there is, then I guess that's it for another week," Oliver said,

"Actually, something has been weighing on my mind," started Alice. When Oliver nodded for her to continue, she laid it out. "It looks like we're increasing the number of kilos we're allowing people to share and that is bringing us in some money, but it's not nearly enough for the size of the business and it's not increasing very quickly. I'm worried that we'll burn through whatever capital we have, and we'll have to restructure. And it's usually last on, first off when it comes to redundancies."

Oliver nodded, smiling. "Yeah, I brought up the same thing when I started. The good news is that we're still a start-up and Richard has deep pockets to fund us until we can become profitable. He's happy enough to keep pumping money into the company. I think there are strategic benefits to him funding SpareSpace. I vaguely recall him saying something about the value of SpareSpace not being in terms of making more than it costs to keep running, but the benefit to society as a whole, with fewer greenhouse emissions from unutilised logistics space."

"Straight out of the employee guide, that phrase," Alice said with a wry grin. 'Well, if you say we won't go bust any time soon, I guess I'll have to believe you. And Richard does have a bunch of companies, doesn't he? I bet there are some synergies at work somewhere along the line, right?"

The angle of asking how the company made money for purely selfish reasons —avoiding redundancies—seemed to be an innocuous justification for asking questions about income. It certainly didn't raise any red flags, but there were only so many times you could ask and be given the same answer that Richard invests in the company because he believes in it, and we'll eventually get to profitability.

Alice gave up asking and had forgotten about it until she was waiting outside a meeting room for the previous meeting to finish and the two analytics guys came storming out. She watched them head back to their desks and collect their things and head out the door. It was an hour before finishing time, so not incredibly suspicious, but when Richard himself came out of the room after them, she made a mental note to follow up on it. Her meeting went well enough, and she finished for the day and was heading home when she noticed the two analytics guys sitting in the outdoor area of one of the pubs on a side street. The outdoor area was starting to fill up but there were still seats available.

Alice decided to investigate. She went inside and ordered a drink, taking it outside and caught one of the analytics guy's eyes.

"Oh, hey. Sam, right? Alice—I'm new at SpareSpace. Hi Peter. Sorry, am I interrupting?" Their body language said that she was, but she ignored it and barrelled on. "Most people are cool at SpareSpace, but man, Richard takes some getting used to, doesn't he?" She watched carefully for a reaction.

Sam grimaced and Peter rolled his eyes. Their table had two empties along with their half-full pint glasses, so Alice surmised that they had one or two drinks under their belts before she came along. Hopefully, that would loosen their tongues.

Sam was the first. "It's... frustrating, Alice. We've been brought on board to monitor the success of the site, to allow others to make data-driven decisions on which bits of the site we should work on next—to get rid of the pain points—but Richard is always dragging us off on ad-hoc pieces that he wants looked at. I feel— we feel—that we're being whiplashed from one thing to the other and so we can't deliver the work that we're being judged on. It's maddening!"

Peter nodded his agreement. "And we never see any changes made off the back of what he asks us to look at. *And*, and we look like chumps when people like Oliver ask about the analysis that we promised him and now can't deliver."

Alice frowned. "What kind of things does he get you to look at?"

"So, you know that the main shipping companies provide a feed of their capacities? Every day they send us a list of slots they've got available, and we load that into the site and allow people to book the slots themselves."

"Remind me again how Richard persuaded the shipping and courier companies to do that?"

Peter smirked. "He told them that they'd be able to claim green credentials—offset some of their greenhouse emissions. Plus, they get a cut of the revenue. And as far as they're concerned, this is wasted capacity, so they are literally getting something for nothing."

"OK, so back to the question. What's Richard getting you to look at?"

"He's looking for movements in the available slots. And how that stacks up historically and against their competitors. And then we have to go out and get the prices that they're charging as well. We're in an enviable position—we get data from the complete industry and on a daily basis, no less."

Alice thought for a minute. "That does sound like a nice position to be in," she said at last. "You'd think that anyone in that position would be able to take advantage of shortages, bump the price up, and shift their deliveries from slots that are expensive to cheaper slots. Nice."

Sam nodded. "Yes, but we've agreed not to be in that business. It makes no sense."

Alice thought she saw the opportunity that the others didn't. Richard wouldn't have to take advantage of that information by being in the transport industry himself. All he would have to do is sell the insight on an ad hoc basis. She shook her head. Surely it couldn't be that easy.

" Let's see if I've got this right. All the courier companies and shipping companies give SpareSpace a list of their spare capacity. Things like hey, we've got a half-empty truck going from London to Bath on the 18th of December. It can take 20kgs. Then SpareSpace allows people to search for that route and date. And lo, that slot comes up and they say, 'Yes please, book it'. And SpareSpace charges them something cheaper than what the courier company would charge. So the user comes out ahead. And the courier company gets paid something for that 20kg hole in their truck that would otherwise not get paid for. And SpareSpace gets paid for connecting the two. And everybody basks in the warmth of being ecologically responsible. How am I doing so far?"

The other two nodded in agreement.

"As a result of this, SpareSpace is sitting on information which is incredibly valuable because it amounts to the aggregate of all the shipping capacity in the country. And anyone in the industry would kill for that information because it allows prices to be perfectly optimised. If you know that nobody can take things from London to Bath in the week before Christmas, then you can afford to put your price up. If you can see that everyone has capacity between Liverpool and Manchester on a particular week, you can lower your price accordingly to get all the business."

"But remember, SpareSpace has agreed not to do that optimisation piece ourselves."

"Good point. Very good point," agreed Alice, taking another sip of her drink. Well, that explained the question of how the business would be able to stay afloat with such a poor business model. It did mean that Richard was less of an ecological entrepreneur than he made out in his marketing and PR though. Kind of cynical making money off data that the suppliers actually gave you in the first place. And doubly so making out that it was all about saving the planet.

She finished her drink and made some more small talk with the guys before making her excuses and heading home. She ducked into the local supermarket to pick up some fresh pasta and sauce for dinner and was waiting in the early evening line for the self-service kiosk and trying hard not to listen to the conversations ahead and behind her in the queue.

"What is this, Berlin in 1945? Yes, there were no artichoke hearts to be had at all. I did ask, I did. And—no we'll just have to try something else." To distract herself from the conversation further, Alice examined the newspapers on the racks beside her. Every single one had Boris on the front page. "REGENT STREET HERO SUSPENDED FOR BREAKING THE RULES" screamed one headline. "COPPER COMES A PROPER CROPPER," shouted another. Alice grabbed the one closest and read the news. Apparently, the investigation into Boris's conduct had been completed and they'd found him wanting for involving her in the case. They mentioned her by name, and she felt her face colouring as she turned to the continuation of the story on the inside pages.

"Excuse me, miss, you're next," an apologetic voice from behind said. She looked up distractedly and noticed that the artichoke woman was gone and a large gap beckoned between her and the kiosks. She waved vaguely at the young man behind her, and the queue leapfrogged her as she dived into the paper.

The internal pages had more photos, one a grainy shot that the paparazzi had managed to get of Boris as he left the station when he'd been told of the investigation. He'd looked terrible. Alice got out her phone and rang him.

"Hello, Alice," he croaked.

"Oh my god, Boris, I'm so sorry."

"Yeah, it's not the best. But as my union rep said, my history of service might help in the investigation."

"I feel responsible," Alice said. "I had no idea that this would happen."

"I knew the rules, Alice. It's not your fault. I took a risk to save lives and it's my responsibility. The wife and I have talked about a few cutbacks we can make, so we're not going to starve. Fewer trips to Costa Bravo maybe. I'll be fine."

It broke Alice's heart to hear the hollowness in Boris's voice. "Well, let me know if there is anything I can do to help," she managed weakly. "Or if you wanted to talk about it over a drink or something," she really wasn't very good at this at all.

"I'll do that, thanks for your call, Alice. I appreciate it. Goodbye." He rang off.

Alice hung up. As she put her phone away, she noticed that Richard had rung her and left a message. Apparently, according to the recent calls record, it had been while she had been in the pub with Sam and Peter. She listened to the message. "Alice, Richard here. Could I see you first thing in the morning tomorrow? Thanks, bye." Short and sweet. Alice's first worry was that he'd somehow been butt dialled while the three of them had been talking about him. That would be typical, him hearing the entire conversation. But thankfully unlikely. Still, what *was* that about?

EXILE

Richard wasted no time in telling Alice what was on his mind.

"I've had a word with the team and, by all accounts, you're doing well. You're slaying the parts that they're giving you and your code is easy to integrate into root, whatever that means. I've got a new challenge for you, if you're up for it?"

Alice nodded, happy to have the boss's praise.

"I've just taken over a small software house to get the IP in an innovative piece of software that they've built, and I need someone with a good fresh knowledge of our systems and processes to go over and help integrate it into our stack. It'll require being over in their offices for about a month or two. I'll get Jacky to give you the details, who to ask for and where their offices are but, if I can get you over there on Monday, that would be great. There are a couple of their team who will be leaving with the takeover, so the sooner you get over there the better."

Alice was a little surprised that he was getting her to handle this. "Are you sure you don't want someone who has been here a little longer to handle the integration side of things?"

He looked surprised. "No, I think you're the best person for the job. I have faith in your abilities. Was there something else?"

"Uh, no. I guess I'll start on Monday."

Richard's tone and words reminded her of someone. It wasn't until she was reporting this new development to Mike via text message that she realised that was the exact approach that Mike had taken in getting her onboard. 'I have faith in your abilities.' She didn't know if that meant that they had attended the same management seminar or course and used that skill on everyone, or whether there was something about her in particular that made managers use that particular angle. She didn't feel bad about it either way—just curious whether it was something in common between Richard and Mike, or something about her.

She didn't get a response from Mike and so didn't know whether the situation was a move in a good or bad direction. Did it mean Richard suspected her and was moving her away from something which he didn't want her to discover, or was she gaining trust and therefore this was proof that they valued her abilities?

On Monday, she tracked down the office tucked away in the basement of an office block opposite London Bridge station. It was still technically close enough to walk from the Barbican, Google saying it would take thirty minutes. But Alice found the streets around Bank to be narrow and congested with pedestrian traffic heading the opposite way and so was fifteen minutes late at the other end.

She descended into the bowels of the office building, a dry cleaner tucked away at the opposite end of the corridor. As she walked through the door of the office, a bored receptionist looked up. She must have been twenty at most and had a lovely mocha complexion which made guessing her ethnicity difficult. Was she a light-skinned black girl or a tanned white one?

"Hi, I'm Alice. I'm here to see Thomas."

"I'll just call him for you." The receptionist had no accent to help place her. She picked up the phone and let Thomas know that Alice was there. Alice looked around. There was no couch or waiting area, just a counter for the receptionist, a vase with a colourful bouquet, and a narrow gap through to the rest of the office space. Through the gap she could make out an open-plan office, but whereas SpareSpace's open-plan office had been gleaming and clean and new, with floor-to-ceiling windows overlooking the street, here there were no windows and the furniture looked decidedly more lived in.

An impish looking man of average height and medium build came to the counter. He had a ready grin and red hair cut short but stylishly. He extended his hand as he approached.

"Hi Alice, I'm Thomas," he said as they shook hands. "Let's go through to my office." He led her back through the gap, skirting the edge of the open-plan office which was really just a single large wooden desk with chipped edges with four computers facing each other, two a side. All four seats were occupied and the young men facing her watched as she walked by, the other two trying to do the same without making it obvious—which of course made it all the more obvious.

There were four closed offices opening onto the main open office space, and Thomas led Alice into the largest one of these. It was about half the size of the area holding four coders. The sumptuous desk chair behind a sizable desk was in stark contrast to the spartan guest chair, and Alice smiled inwardly at the barely hidden psychological game in play. Behind the chair was a bookshelf with assorted folders and technical books on various programming languages.

"We'll get you introduced to the team soon enough, but I just wanted to give you a feel for who we are and what we do here." Alice settled into her seat and smiled encouragingly. "Richard has said that we'll be able to operate independently which is the only reason I accepted his investment."

"I thought he bought you out?" Alice asked.

Thomas frowned. "Oh, no, he just bought out my previous investor." Alice was finding it hard to tell how old Thomas was. He had a preternaturally young appearance, but when he smiled the lines around his eyes were too exaggerated for him to be in his late twenties as she had originally thought. Maybe early thirties? "We've created a rather impressive CMS," continued Thomas. "It's lightweight and smart with a great GUI, and we're going to take on WordPress."

Alice frowned a little at this news. A CMS was a content management system —basically a website that allowed user logins and interaction.

WordPress was the biggest CMS in the world, primarily because it was free, so it would be interesting to see how they thought they would be able to make money competing with free. The interface that users used to input the data and manipulate what the blog would look like was the GUI and maybe that was where they'd be able to drive a point of difference. Such an obviously bad business proposition didn't strike Alice as being a particularly good enterprise to take over—which meant that either Richard had made an error or there was something more going on here.

"Tell me more about the CMS," she said.

Thomas then proceeded to give her a five-minute spiel on the features of their CMS and how it was better than anything else on the market. She let him talk, hoping he'd get to an actual feature that wasn't common across all the other CMSs that she knew about. He trailed off eventually, mistaking her silence for rapt attention. "As you can see, we've got something special here. Definitely something SpareSpace will find valuable."

"Cool, I'm sure," she replied. "Now, about the team?"

"Oh, yeah. We have the coders out there. We'll get to them soon. In the office beside me is the Art Director and her team, in those two other offices are our new account managers. And you've already met Dolly at reception."

"So, do you just have the CMS as a product?"

"Oh no, we primarily make websites. That's why we built the CMS—to make it easier and quicker to make the websites. That way we can do more and more, in much less time than it normally takes to put together a website. Great business model, right?"

"Definitely," Alice responded, more because it seemed to be expected of her than out of any genuine enthusiasm for what he had said. "And which provider do you use to host the websites on the cloud?"

Thomas looked surprised. "Oh, we don't put anything on the cloud—we host our own infrastructure. More control, see."

Now it was Alice's turn to be surprised, and she couldn't keep that surprise off her face or out of her voice. "Oh, you want all that hassle of patching servers and replacing the hardware?"

Thomas wrinkled his nose. "Control! We can finetune the performance of the server and maximise the availability and response times. C'mon, I'll introduce you to Wayne." He got up and led the way back to the desks. He stood beside a short squat man with a comically full beard. "This is Wayne," he told her. "He takes care of our infrastructure. Wayne, this is Alice. Can you give her the low down of what we do and then hand her off to PB?"

"Sure," said Wayne, smiling a greeting at Alice. "Pull up a chair," he told her, and she looked around for one. Nothing. "Oh, the crayon crowd had a meeting with a client and haven't returned them. David, can you go and get our guest a chair?"

David turned out to be the tall thin guy sitting opposite Wayne. "No can do, Wayne. I'm under the hammer for the Belsen account. Maybe Rahul could do it?" he said with a Polish accent.

Rahul looked up. He was from South Asia, slim and short. "I'm a little busy, myself. PB?"

PB looked around. "Where did she go?"

Alice came back, rolling a chair behind her. She'd seen the likely outcome of the discussion and rather than wait for the four of them to bounce the responsibility between them she'd knocked on the door of the office and asked if they were using one of the spare chairs, then helped herself. "Cool, now where were we?"

Wayne pointed to one of his screens. "This is where I monitor the performance of our server—the traffic and hits and that sort of thing." The screen was split in half, showing a line graph in each part. The top one was pretty consistent, at about two-thirds of the y axis, bubbling along with the odd blip. The bottom one was a more extreme set of data. Typically, it tracked along at about 5% of the y axis except for a block where it shot up to 100% and stayed there, before dropping back to normal. She could see that the time period involved was for the previous Friday.

"What's the bottom graph?"

"That's our internet usage, it's just a chart our ISP set up so we don't tend to take much notice of it."

"What happened there?" she asked, pointing to the 100% blip.

"Oh, we went on an offsite last Friday," explained Wayne. Alice waited. That was about all he was going to say on the matter.

"OK, so why did the internet max out on the day that everybody was at an offsite?" she asked.

Wayne looked uncomfortable. "Well, we didn't *all* go to the offsite. We left one person behind to look after the place and respond if anything happened like a site going down or a service needing restarting."

Alice couldn't understand why they wouldn't tell her more. She glanced around. Rahul and David looked bemused but turned their attention back to their own screens. PB had found something on his screen which was very important and was intensely focused on it. He was white, skinny and average height. He had fine features and wore the wisp of a moustache and the suggestion of a tuft of hair on his chin. He was starting to blush a little.

Alice decided to return to the subject later and instead asked Wayne questions about the number of clients they had, how many websites they hosted and how many used their CMS. She found that she had to ask a couple of times to get the information that she wanted, Wayne needing the questions phrased just right for him to deliver the answers that Alice was looking for. She couldn't figure out if he was on the autistic spectrum and needed a certain pattern of language used or whether he was being willingly obtuse. She suspected the latter but wasn't sure if it was because she was a woman, an outsider or both. Eventually, she'd learned what she could from Wayne and rolled next door to Rahul.

PB and David stood up and headed for the door. Rahul smiled at her questioning face.

"Smokers," he said.

Wayne stood up and headed through to the kitchenette in the corner. A table with a basket of snacks stood beside a full-sized fridge and a kitchen bench with a coffee machine on it. Wayne started making himself a cup of tea and Alice made use of the sudden privacy to find out about the spike in internet traffic the previous Friday.

"So, what really happened last Friday?" she asked casually, lowering her voice a little to ensure no one overheard.

Rahul seemed delighted to have been asked, looking around quickly before answering. "We left PB behind—he volunteered—while we went out for a team-building session. We come back and Wayne looks at the logs. PB had set up a bunch of scripts and was downloading shit loads of porn, all sorts of sites, all the videos they had and putting them in zip files on his personal cloud storage. Pretty much from the second we stepped out the door to the second he left for the day—flatlined the traffic. That's why he's PB—it's short for Porn Boy. His real name is Aaron."

Alice smiled but held a hand in front of her face. "That's terrible," she grinned. "Did he get in trouble? Surely he'd be fired? Disciplinary action?"

Rahul shook his head at each question. "That's not quite the way things are done around here," he told her.

Alice frowned and blinked twice. Wayne returned with his cup of tea. "So, tell me about the code base for the CMS," she said to Rahul.

Rahul filled her in on the languages used and the code base for the CMS. All the while she kept alert for some nuance or facet of the CMS which would differentiate it from the competitors in the market. Nothing came up, so she got him to let her know which of the customer base he supported. He listed those he had helped in the past and mentioned that with the new account managers that he hadn't talked to any customers for a couple of weeks. Which was good because it let him concentrate on the coding side of things.

The smokers came back, PB smelling faintly of raspberries, while David smelt strongly of tobacco. She spent some time with each, learning about the customers each of them supported and the kind of things that they did. When she was satisfied with her knowledge of the technical side of things, she decided to expand her knowledge of the wider team and returned to the room where she had fetched her chair from.

"Hi, thanks for the chair, I thought I'd stop by for a chat and introduce myself properly. Do you have time for a coffee?"

There were two people in the office. One, a young woman in her late twenties, tall, slim and good looking in an understated way. The other was a tall man of similar age of some Pacific Island extraction, thickly built and looking every part the rugby player with a distinct lack of a neck. He looked up as she entered, but the woman was the one who rose and rather imperiously announced that she was going to have her break. She was dressed very fashionably, accentuating both height and slimness with a flowing black dress perfectly accessorized with thick black obsidian beads and a wide belt. The femininity of the ensemble was offset with a pair of chunky Doc Martens and an assortment of bangles on one arm and a sinuous gold arm cuff on the other. Faced with such effortless style, Alice was a little intimidated. She felt a little out of place beside her, dressed as she was in her typical office garb of jeans, faded T-shirt and the plaid long-sleeved shirt over the top. Even her battered sneakers which she normally thought were casual-chic now struck her as just scruffy.

"I'm Victoria," she said as she floated by.

"Alice!" Alice found herself calling out her name as she tried to catch up.

She followed Victoria back up the stairs to street level and across the street into the station. Alice was surprised when they approached one of the chain coffee shops. Were they here ironically? Or was it cool to like the chain coffee shops now? Just this one, or all of them? Alice thought herself lucky not to have to waste any brainpower or memory to monitor the coolness of such things and joined Victoria in the queue. They did not have to wait long and the barista across the counter greeted Victoria like a long-lost friend, kissing her on both cheeks and conversing for a bit in rapid-fire French. She had apparently ordered and turned towards Alice, the barista waiting likewise. Alice stammered out her order and with a farewell, Victoria led her to one of the high stools at the window bench.

"Don't you have to wait at the counter?" asked Alice.

Victoria settled herself on the stool and mentioned that Stefan would bring their drinks to them.

"So, what has Thomas got himself into this time?" Victoria started.

"What do you mean?"

"Well, first of all, he gets into bed with the brewers, nice dash of cash, thank you very much. Hire some account managers because underneath it all our Thomas is a coder, and all he wants to do is code. No time for dealing with customers, nope. Just code, code, code. So, he gets investment, gets some account managers so none of the coders need to talk to customers. Then he notices that the sales funnel is running low—all the work that the current customer base needs is all in the first half of the year. It makes the sales look great and makes the brewer happy to get into bed with us, but all of a sudden he's looking at an increased cost base with the account managers and a sales number which is frozen."

"How do you know all of this?"

"Thomas is a dear, but he's very sharing. Especially on Fridays."

"What happens on Fridays?"

"Well, the coders, and Phil my designer, they all stay late and drink beer and play computer games. The office turns into an internet cafe."

"And Thomas plays as well?"

"Oh no, we have a nice glass of chardonnay and chat about the business. Occasionally one of the account managers will stay as well, but usually it's just the two of us. I wouldn't say he uses me as a sounding board because he never asks me what he should do, but he talks at me, like he's thinking his next move over as he does so. I'm happy enough because I hear what's going on before it happens so I think I should know when the business is getting into trouble. So that I can make my plans accordingly."

"So, when does SpareSpace get involved?"

"The month-end management meeting happens on a Thursday night and so on Friday Thomas is a little more pensive and so I ask what happened. Turns out he had to show the board the numbers including the forecasts for the next six months and there were a few words said. Like the brewers weren't expecting there to be nothing in the sales funnel. So they said 'we want out' and eventually Thomas found another investor to take their place. SpareSpace."

"Just like that?"

"Just like that. Thomas is one very good salesman. Just not for websites!"

Their coffees appeared like magic, with more kisses and 'a bientot'.

"So now it seems you're here to help integrate the code base into SpareSpace's systems?"

Alice had the feeling there wasn't much that happened that Victoria wasn't aware of. "You certainly have your finger on the pulse," she said.

She looked at Alice over her disposable coffee cup and raised an eyebrow. "You have no idea. It's only a matter of time before Thomas can't sell people on his dream anymore and the whole thing goes belly up."

"So why don't you jump before that happens? Surely it's better to be in control over your own destiny?"

Victoria smiled enigmatically. "Oh, I'm in charge of my own destiny, Alice. Bank on that. Let's just say I'm very interested in exactly how it all pans out. And if I'm wrong, then staying put is the best bet I can make. Shall we head back?"

As they re-entered the office, Alice noticed Dolly the receptionist looking vacant at the front desk. On a whim she slowed, calling out a thanks to Victoria for the coffee, and asked Dolly what she was doing for lunch. Dolly looked surprised but said that she didn't have plans.

"I've always wanted to try Borough Market—shall we see if anything appeals?"

"Oh, there are far fewer shops open on a Monday. We'd be better off on Thursday."

"I can't wait until then, what time do you go to lunch?"

"Whenever really, let me grab my jacket," replied Dolly, already getting to her feet.

They headed back outside, dodging more traffic and more pedestrians, heading to the market under the railway lines and in front of the cathedral. It was a little early for the peak crowds but there was still a large number of people in attendance—an even mix of students, tourists and office workers. The food stands ran the gamut from speciality sausages to frighteningly specific ethnic offerings. Wanting to make a decision quickly, Alice chose a vegetarian baguette from one of the bakers on the square. Dolly got a salami baguette from the same stall and they wandered away from the market along the cobbled streets towards the river, ending up past the Golden Hinde and leaning on the rail beside a cafe.

"So, how long have you been working for Thomas?" asked Alice.

"About a year—it's my first job out of school," replied Dolly.

"Are you enjoying it?"

"I guess it has its moments."

"It's a young company, right? Lots of personalities. I had a coffee with Victoria. She seems nice."

"Victoria? Yeah, she's ok. She hasn't been too happy since Scooter left."

"Oh? Who's Scooter?"

"One of the coders. She and him got on well. He left kind of suddenly— I don't know the details but there was a disagreement between Thomas and him, and so he left. Ever since then she's been a bit miffed. Hard to tell sometimes with her, but I notice things."

"A valuable skill for reception, right?"

Dolly smiled. "Absolutely."

The outdoor seating area beside them had been steadily growing more and more populated with lunchtime patrons wanting to enjoy the views over the Thames while having their food. The rumble of their conversations was making it harder and harder to hear each other, so they finished their respective baguettes, deposited the wrappers in a nearby rubbish bin and started to retrace their steps back to the office.

"Just between you and me, sometimes I wish they were all a little more professional."

"Your colleagues?"

Dolly nodded. "Little things like leaving confidential information on the printer, that sort of thing. And the snack box! Always at least five quid short. It's embarrassing when the guy comes to restock it. One conversation I overheard was 'I only got married because I wanted a blowjob'. What are you supposed to do with that information?"

Alice nodded in sympathy. "It is a young office."

Dolly looked at her sharply. "That was Thomas!"

"Oh. Is there any sexual harassment in the office?"

Dolly thought for a minute. "No, nothing like that. The guys are more like brothers. Maybe some inappropriate jokes and teasing. I get more of a creepy vibe from one of the visitors that Thomas has been meeting with."

They had made their way back to the office by now, Dolly returning to her position behind the desk.

"Oh?" asked Alice.

"Yeah, weaselly looking guy—perfect suit. Leery eyes. Someone named Johan Bernier."

SECRETS

Alice thanked Dolly for coming with her to lunch and then headed back inside as the name bounced around her head, ringing bells. She headed into the kitchenette to make herself a cup of tea to fill in time while she racked her brain for where she had heard that name before. She couldn't place the name but the mental image of a weasel in a suit with leery eyes certainly made her remember Richard's lawyers at the SpareSpace offices. If Richard was taking over or even investing in Thomas's company then it made sense that the same lawyer would be talking to both people.

Alice frowned into her tea. There were too many loose threads. She couldn't figure it out herself. Maybe she needed to talk to someone to make sense of it all. She still had half a day left in their office—maybe something else would come to light. She weighed up questioning Thomas, but it didn't really match her mandate from Richard. She was there to integrate code, not haul the co-owner over the coals. She headed back to the desk with the coders and pulled her chair around to sit beside PB.

"Hi! I'm Alice. I'm helping SpareSpace integrate your CMS into their tech stack and naturally enough I have some questions. Do you have a few minutes to go through it?"

"Sure, what would you like to know?"

"How long have you been working here?"

"I'm one of the long-timers," PB responded. "Originally it was me, Thomas, Scooter and Wayne."

"Oh! So, who actually coded the CMS?"

"Well, most of us have added functionality to it over the years, but the bulk of the work was done by me and Scooter."

Alice looked around theatrically. "Which one is Scooter?" she asked, as if she didn't know the answer.

"He doesn't work here anymore. He left about three months ago."

"That must have been a loss—he must have known how it all worked."

"The code is well commented actually, so it's quite clear how it all works."

Alice smiled. "So, you couldn't say which bits Scooter wrote and which bits other people did?"

PB frowned. "I don't know why you would need to, but I guess not. This was before we used any form of version control, so all the code just got released to production."

Alice nodded. A picture was forming in her head of the work that was in front of her. The code for the CMS would be easy to integrate into the SpareSpace system. All they would have to do is to ensure that the user management worked from one code base to the other and that would be it. Simple. Maybe a week's work at the very most with comprehensive testing. Hardly worth sending her over here, really. Which meant that it was a fool's errand. Richard wanted her out of the SpareSpace offices for some reason. Alice thought for a second. Richard wouldn't go to the lengths of buying a software house just to get her out of the office. But if he wanted her gone for a time, and he'd already bought the software company, then that might make a convenient excuse. If he didn't want her in the office, then maybe that's where she should be? She looked up. PB and the others were all watching her.

"Sorry—I zoned out," she explained. "I've got another appointment," she said as she stood up. "Thanks for all your help." She headed out the door, saying goodbye to Dolly and weighing up fighting her way through the commuters at the station to get to the offices quickly, before electing to get some more sun by walking through the centre of the city.

As she walked, she summarised what she knew so that she could report it concisely to Mike. Richard told her that he trusted her, but that meant nothing. He wanted her to integrate the CMS into the SpareSpace systems. That was ludicrously simple and straightforward and didn't need anyone with special skills. So, sending her to the London Bridge offices must have been to get her out of the SpareSpace office. What the lawyers were doing there and what Scooter and his leaving had to do with anything, she didn't know or care about. None of that had anything to do with The Handler. The sunshine had brought out the office workers and every green area along her route was crowded with people eating lunch and soaking up as much sunshine as they could before returning to the glow of the fluorescent tubes.

When she got back to the office, she couldn't see anything out of the ordinary. She had half expected to find a secretive meeting taking place in one of the offices, or a VIP being escorted in or out of the building by dark-suited security guards with earpieces to a waiting SUV. Instead, she saw Richard crossing the office and, noticing her approach, swing towards her with a smile.

"Ah, you're back! Excellent, how long do you think it will take to integrate?"

She smiled back. 'Only about a week."

Richard's smile froze. "A week? For the whole encryption system? And plugging it into the distributed message system? That doesn't sound right."

Alice frowned. "Encryption? Distributed message system? Nobody mentioned those. Thomas talked about the CMS, but nothing else."

Richard was still for a second before he pulled out his mobile phone and made a call. "Hi, Thomas, Richard here. I'm talking to Alice and she says you didn't discuss the encryption system. I'll remind you that funding was very specifically provided so that we could integrate that IP into our systems. So, I'll ask very politely—what the fuck is going on?" There was a pause while Thomas responded, his voice barely audible to Alice. It went on for a while, Richard's frown deepening as it did so. "Can I just interrupt you there, Thomas? If it's in a different system, why didn't you show Alice? Tell you what, I don't care. I'm sending Alice back. If she can't get access to the system you told me about, I'm withdrawing my funding and unleashing my lawyers." Another pause, the pleading tone of Thomas now detectable. "That's not what you told me—you said it was totally operational." Pause. "That's better. Alice will come back tomorrow morning, do let me know if I should send the lawyers with her." And with that, he hung up.

"Our friend Thomas may have made an exaggerated claim about some of the functionality that his CMS has got. If the encryption system exists, I need to know. If it's only partly built, that's OK, I just need to know how far along it is. And when we might expect it. My concern here is that it's vapourware. That it doesn't exist, and it's just a bullshit carrot to dangle in order to get funding. So, I need you to be my eyes and ears and find out all you can about the encryption system—whether it's real, where it is and when I can get it." Richard's face was a mask of intensity and the hand that held his phone was white, but his voice was all control, the syllables enunciated clearly and clipped. "Go home now—we need to give him time but get there early tomorrow. Let me know how you get on and tell me if you need me to do anything to help."

Alice nodded, turned on her heel and headed back out the door. Clocking off early as a contractor meant losing hours of paid work, but as a salaried employee being told to go home early was great! Although her concise summary for Mike was going to need to be a lot more complex. As she made her way back home, she texted the update to Mike and hit send. She needed more time to ponder what she'd just discovered, so instead of going straight up to Zoltan's apartment, she sat in the park next door and thought about it. The children in the school next door were screaming and running around, but her brain treated it like white noise, so she was effectively alone.

She knew that historically cryptography had been a race between those wanting privacy and those wanting to discover what people were doing. Typically, in races like that the use of technology helped one side and then the other, a constant one-upmanship which led to unexpected technological advances. Periodically, though, someone would cheat.

An example of this was in World War Two. The Germans had a very secure technology called Enigma which utilised the technology of the time. The Allies pretty much had to invent the modern computer to break the code in time to use the contents of the messages each day. After that, improvements in codes were followed by improvements in the technology to break them. Brute force efforts—effectively trying every single combination of characters as a password—would now take centuries. And so, instead, malicious operators (usually governments) started insisting that encrypted systems include a backdoor for them to gain direct access to the messages. And other malicious actors (usually criminals) would trick people into installing programs that would allow access to the computers remotely. Sometimes this ability was hidden within other computer programs.

Most email and other message systems were encrypted, so if anyone wanted to look over your shoulder at your messages, they would have to have compromised the software you used or your computer via a program installed on it, or else just had access to the actual computer itself. Until something called Quantum Computing came about, anyway. Alice wasn't an expert on codes and such, but what she had pieced together was that a new class of computers was in development where the technological advantage currently enjoyed by the encryptors would be obliterated by processing power so advanced that the trillions of years it would currently take to brute force the passwords would now take eight hours. Well, that was the theory anyway—these Quantum Computers weren't exactly being made by Dell and sold at Currys just yet!

The school released a tidal wave of Die Kinder, a screaming shrieking deluge of kids, some accompanied by parents. *Time to go*, thought Alice as the park began to fill. She went home and enjoyed a forgettable night in front of the TV, alone because Zoltan was spending a week on the continent on a yacht holiday in the Adriatic with friends. That night Alice had a nightmare that barely needed interpreting. She was about to walk along a spider's web of many different layers, a spider on each watching her. One looked like Mike, another like Richard, a third like Thomas and the fourth had a weasel's head on a fuzzy tarantula-like eight-legged body. She had to make her way across the web and whenever she took a step the spider would lunge towards her, making it a nerve-racking choice of where to place her next step to keep ahead of the spiders. She woke up in a sweat berating Dream-Alice for not working out a more elegant solution. Her dream-self had taken a step on each web in turn, which kept the wall of spiders breathing down her neck. Awake-Alice was angry that Dream-Alice hadn't run along one web until the spider was just behind her and then switched to a different web. Less switching and more efficient.

She made her way into the London Bridge office, arriving a bit before 8am, the walk being considerably quicker with fewer besuited bankers and lawyers up that early. Dolly was just arriving as she got there and the lights were already on inside, so at least someone was working hard. Dolly saw her looking over at the lights and let her know that Victoria and Thomas usually beat her into the office. Smiling her thanks for that news, Alice headed through to Thomas' office. She knocked on the door and headed in.

Thomas was sitting on his power-play office chair and, as he turned, she got a glimpse of the real Thomas, a worried look with harrowed eyes, before the beaming-smile mask returned. He was all enthusiasm as he greeted her. "Hi Alice, welcome back to the office. Sorry about the misunderstanding."

Alice waited for him to fill her in on the misunderstanding. And waited. "So, about the encryption?" she asked, sitting in the guest chair.

He shuffled uncomfortably. "Well, here's the thing," he started. "We do have a great encryption system, it's brilliant. The only thing is that it hasn't been fully written yet."

"OK, let me know who's writing it for you, I'll have a look at the spec, we'll talk about the plan for delivery and then I can report back to Richard."

"That's just it," said Thomas, spreading his hands in front of him.

"There's no plan. The code is all in someone's head."

"OK, well that's not good. What if something happens to that person? Still, not the end of the world. Who is it? PB? Rahul?"

There was an awkward silence. "Scooter."

Alice frowned. "I thought he'd left?" she managed.

Thomas wrung his hands. "Yes, that's right he has. But while he was here, while he was a full-time permanent employee, he was working on the project in his own time, so therefore we have ownership of the intellectual property."

Alice's frown twisted into confusion. "You mean he was working on his project at work? On company equipment? During his work day?"

"Uh... no, no, he was working on it at his home on his own equipment. But that doesn't matter. The law states that when you hire a coder as a permanent employee, you own all the coding work he does, whether it's at his place on his equipment or in the office on your equipment."

The penny dropped for Alice. "Ah, and when you told Scooter of this, he told you to kick rocks."

"Kick rocks?"

"Kick rocks, pound sand, get stuffed. He didn't want to play ball."

"Ah yes. He was quite... colourful with his disagreement. I was forced to bring in my lawyers and when they said that they couldn't help me, they recommended a different firm. They have been most helpful, but Scooter has been most uncooperative. I think we will have to go to court, which will take forever."

"And how complete is the code? Do you have any of it at all? Could someone here finish it? Maybe you could buy it off Scooter? Or invest in him so that he can complete it quicker? Surely 50% of something is better than 100% of nothing?"

Thomas looked at her for a while, and then arched his neck and checked to see if anyone was in the office behind her. He got up and walked around to pull the door closed. He returned to his desk and sat back down. The smile was gone now.

"What Scooter showed me was very exciting. What do you know about cryptography?"

"Some."

"OK, I'll give you the basic version. So, when you want to stop people from looking at your messages online you encrypt them, right? It's what the little padlock on your browser means—its saying that your connection is secure. The contents of the website have been locked before sending it to you and then unlocked at the other end so that you can see the contents. Now the key that locks the message is important. The bigger the key the more secure it is, right? The longer it would take to break it. And, at the moment, for the standard keys we use, they would take trillions of years to break. And somehow Scooter managed to use the human genome as a key."

"Huh?" said Alice. "The human what now?"

"The human genome. You've heard about DNA, right? Seen pictures of a double helix? That's the code which makes you. If you had a lab and someone's DNA you could grow another one of them. They would look pretty much the same as you, and they would have the same hereditary problems as you, but they would obviously be twenty or thirty years younger than you and have a totally different personality than you. You can't speed up their growth rate just yet, so think of them as being a spookily closely resembling daughter rather than a twin."

"Gotcha: DNA is the blueprint for you."

"So, the genome is splitting the helix and writing down the code there. Very tricky computer work. Two huge problems. First of all, when you take the sample, you can have errors which means you don't have an accurate picture of the code. Think of it like blurring in a picture. So that's easy— you take another picture. The blurring will eventually cancel itself out, and you'll have a clear picture of the DNA. You might need a few shots, but you get the idea. The other problem is that while the recipe for Alice is very long, a lot of it is rubbish. Filler. Stuff that is the same as a banana or a chimpanzee. The bit that makes Alice human is a small proportion of the code, and the bit that makes Alice, Alice, is even smaller again. It's about 700MB for the whole thing but about 4MB for the Alice part."

Alice frowned. "So, if you use the DNA as a key, like sticking your finger into a lock, then you'd need to do it a few times because you might not get an accurate reading. And, even then, while the key length is very long you're only getting a 4MB key?"

Thomas smiled, nodding. "I should say that while it's 'only' 4MB, that's still two *thousand* times longer than the current length of keys that are used normally."

Alice's eyes widened. If Quantum Computers were the leap forward in cracking codes that would take 8 hours to brute force a lock, then using this DNA as a key would swing things back in favour of those wanting to lock things securely. 8 hours times 2000 would mean that it would take close to 2 years to crack a lock even with a Quantum Computer. She nodded to herself. Secure communication for a criminal mastermind in another country would be essential. She fancied that she could smell The Handler's interest. And that explained Richard being involved. And probably the lawyers' involvement as well. "And what about the distributed message system?"

"Scooter's system wasn't just about encrypting messages, but also distributing the messages themselves."

"Huh? That makes no sense."

Thomas was quiet for a few seconds. "Alice, how do you watch programs on TV? Movies?"

Alice frowned. She wasn't about to tell Thomas about all the streaming sites that she knew about where she could watch what she liked when she liked. "Um... Netflix?"

Thomas nodded like that was the answer he expected. "Ok, you're probably too young to know about this. Before Netflix put a good front end and search on their media library and charged a subscription for it, there wasn't any legitimate place that would allow you to watch things online. Oh, some studios allowed you to stream a show if you paid for it, but there wasn't a central place for *all* your media needs. So, some tech people put together something called torrents."

"Torrents?"

"Yeah. You'd install a torrent client and point it at a folder on your computer. All the files in that folder would become available to other users of the same type of client. And if someone wanted a copy of that file on your computer, they would start downloading it. Now the clever thing that the torrent client did was to split the file up. And even more clever was that if anyone else had that file in their folder, then the torrent client would figure out who was the best person to download the file parts from. So, the file was actually distributed across the network. The theory being that no one person actually shared the file—person A shared two parts, person B shared three and person C shared four parts. If the law asked where you got the file from, what are you going to say? No one person gave you the file. Then, for a variety of reasons, primarily that the legit media industry provided a usable paid alternative, the torrents started to decrease. It didn't help that you could put files infected with viruses and trojans into your folder."

"Got it."

"Scooter is so clever. He took that to the next level. He made a communication network that sends files to all the nodes. So, if you have five people using his program, and person A wants to send a message to person B, the file with the message gets split into say three parts and sent to all of the four other people."

"What's to stop the other people from opening it?"

"They're encrypted and those other people don't know how to unlock it."

"Won't that build up a lot of unused messages after a while?"

"Yes, but there are periodic purges."

Alice pursed her lips. "I'd still be worried that someone would eventually decode the messages to me that were sitting on someone else's computer."

Thomas cocked his head. "That's why the encryption part is so important. And apparently he made a setting so that you could ensure that each other person would only get a partial set of the message."

"How would that work?"

"Person A wants to send the message to person B. So the system breaks your message into ten parts. Each person gets sent three of the parts selected at random. And the nodes keep sending parts that they receive to a random selection of the other nodes."

Alice shook her head. "That doesn't scale. The more people you have in the network, the more sharing you have and the longer you have to wait to get the full message. And you don't know how long you have to keep passing on the messages before you're guaranteed to have a full collection of all the pieces of the message."

Thomas nodded. "You are right, of course. It's incredibly inefficient, but two things he pointed out to me when I raised the same concerns. First of all, it's impossible to run any network analysis on the pattern the messages take—all nodes get a constant stream of traffic. Second of all, it's impossible to block. As long as there is a node in the network broadcasting, you'll eventually get the message. And in terms of scaling, it was never intended to be for everyone."

"Let me guess—you don't have that code either?"

Thomas looked very tired. "You can see why I'm so keen on getting Scooter's code, right?"

Alice looked at him without smiling. "You've told someone rich and powerful that you've got something which you don't have. What do you think he'll do when he finds out?"

"You can't tell him. Look out there," he said, indicating the office. "All of them will lose their jobs. I'll lose my house."

"How did the lawyers get involved?"

"I told you, Scooter wouldn't acknowledge our legitimate interests in his code."

"No, I mean, why those particular lawyers?"

"They were referred by my lawyers. It was a bit strange. My firm was very keen on going after Scooter, but then it was like they had second thoughts. They found a different firm to handle the case though, a more expensive firm, but I would only have to pay my original lawyer's rates. So, I was coming out ahead. And they seem good."

"I'm going to have to tell Richard something soon, aren't I? What should I tell him, do you think? I'm not going to lie to him for you. So what did you imagine that you would tell him when he found out?"

"I rather thought—hoped—I hoped that I would have the matter resolved by that time. It's just taken a little longer than I expected. If only he wasn't so damned stubborn. The law is on my side you understand—he doesn't have a leg to stand on."

"And yet here we are," responded Alice, getting to her feet and leaving Thomas's office.

SCOOTER

Alice didn't go far, heading next door to Victoria's office.

"Good morning," she said as Victoria looked up.

Victoria was dressed in what could only be described as 'alt-girl chic', with a black party dress worn over a long-sleeved T-shirt and jeans. Her accessories, as always, made the outfit—a collar and wide-brimmed hat worn so far back that it looked like a halo. Alice found herself thinking that when she grew up that's how she wanted to dress.

"Good morning," smiled Victoria. Darker lipstick and smouldering eyeshadow. Maybe more 'goth-girl chic'?

"Do you have a minute?"

Victoria shrugged. "Sure."

Alice pulled up a chair. "So, I heard Scooter left the company. That's a pity, I heard you two were close?"

Victoria shrugged again. "I guess, he's cool."

"I was wondering if you could arrange a meeting?"

"With you and him? Why would I do that?"

"I need to talk to him and if I tell him who I am, he'll think it's about the legal situation."

"And it isn't?"

"And it is not."

Victoria thought for a few seconds. "Tell you what, you give me your details and I'll forward them to him. If he's keen, he'll get in touch."

Alice didn't like that idea. She could be waiting for days with only Victoria's word that she had even passed the details on. And she wouldn't be able to follow up or nudge or remind. She'd be at a severe disadvantage. But she didn't have any leverage and could think of no better argument to get her own way. Besides, Victoria was intimidating. "Sure, OK," she managed. She gave Victoria her phone number as well as her email address. "It would be cool if he could get in touch soon," she said as she left.

"I'll let him know that," Victoria responded coolly.

Alice thanked her and headed outside. The sun hadn't quite burnt off the low layer of cloud sitting over the city, and there was a slight coolness to the air that had the commuters wondering if it was time to start wearing a jacket, at least early in the morning. She walked past the station and the Shard towards City Hall and the huge paved riverside overlooked by glass-fronted offices. The path from the road to the riverside used to have a fissure cut into it with running water trickling through it connecting to one of the water features. But too many besuited millennials had walked into it or twisted an ankle while looking at their phones and so it had been bricked up, leaving a scar along the pathway. Alice wanted to put enough space between herself and the office where it would be impossible to be overheard or even noticed. She came to the plaza with the City Hall next to the open-air auditorium called the Scoop, noting yet again how it looked like someone had dug out the Scoop and made the town hall out of the excavations—the City Hall looking like the inverse of the auditorium.

She wasted no time mounting the steps and walking along the greenspace behind the hall and sat down under the trees. She pulled out her phone and stared at it for a few minutes, organising her thoughts. She'd been pretty sure she knew what was going on when she made her report to Mike, but this morning had proven that she had only a partial view. She dialled Mike's number. It went straight through to his voicemail, so she left a message asking him to get in touch. Then she waited. It was about 9 in the morning at this stage and she only had a few options in terms of next steps. She wanted to get a steer from Mike about what to do. She had a pretty good view of the people around her, though no one really dallied—

most were office workers on their way to the office. The occasional tourist was on their way to Tower Bridge or was making a short detour from their walk along the riverside, so she had as much privacy as you could expect nestled amongst the touristy centre of a city of more than eight million.

Her phone vibrated in her hand, shocking her. She'd been staring at it, almost daring it to ring and the sudden physical vibration was startling. She looked at the caller ID, and felt a frisson when it read "Caller ID withheld". Maybe this was Scooter!

"Hello, Alice here," she answered.

"Hi Alice, Mike here, what's up?"

"Oh," she said, a little disappointed it wasn't Scooter.

"Nice to hear from you too," responded Mike, a smile detectable down the phone line. "You called?"

Alice collected herself and filled Mike in on what she had found out. When she got to the part of the story where the lawyers were involved, she heard Mike give a short intake of breath and then the line went very quiet. When she had finished, she wasn't sure that he was still there, such was the intense silence on the other end of the line. "Are you there, Mike?"

"Uh... yes, yes, I'm still here. Wow, this is good, I'm really glad that you have made this much progress."

"So, what do I do next?"

'Well, obviously you have to meet with Scooter and find out what you can about the encryption and the distributed message system."

"Yes, I figured out that part, but what do I tell Richard? Do I tell him that Thomas doesn't have the code? Or do I delay?"

"The sooner that you can meet with Scooter the better. We don't want Richard or The Handler to react to being told that the code is not real or won't be delivered. They might do something... permanent." The morning didn't seem quite so warm under the trees anymore.

"Uh... ok, but what do I tell Richard if he presses me?"

"You'll think of something," Mike said nonchalantly. When she didn't respond, he continued. "Look, it doesn't matter—don't answer your mobile. Tell him you need more time. Say that the code needs an extensive installation process. Or a complicated testing routine. Or that it's in a language that you need help with. Or— ooh this is a good one. Tell him that the code is encrypted using its own encryption system and that you need to wait for keys to be generated. That's a circular situation that will mess with his head."

The thought of doing anything short of a good job in the most efficient way filled Alice with dread. She wasn't used to lying, padding of invoices or anything underhand, which made her able to sleep at night and a good contractor, but a lousy spy. "I'll do what I can, Mike. But what does all this mean? How are we going to be able to use this to get to The Handler?"

"I'll put my thinking cap on and try to figure that out. In the meantime, do you have Scooter's full name? We'll see if there's anything else we can use as leverage."

"I'm afraid that's all I've got. I'm not 100% sure that's his actual name to tell you the truth."

"That's ok, we've got the payroll information for the company, so we should be able to track him down that way. This is good, Alice. Keep at it."

"Oh, before you go—Boris. I heard that he got demoted, is there nothing you can do to help him out?"

There was a pause on the other end of the phone. "I understand your attachment to Boris, but you really shouldn't be asking me to interfere with anything involving the judicial system, Alice. Especially when we've been talking about the good work you've been doing helping us with The Handler. An unscrupulous person would equate the two and say that you're setting up a situation where, in exchange for your help, we will help intercede on Boris's behalf. Which is the sort of strictly political situation we don't want to be in. So, no, I couldn't and wouldn't have helped Boris in his review which was handled independently as it should have been by the ICCP. Sorry."

"Oh, sorry, I didn't think—I just think it's sad that he—that we worked so hard in solving that case and got punished for it."

"I understand. But he did break the rules, Alice. Even if he did do it for the right reasons. And I'm not going to get involved in that. But I'll tell you what, I'll keep what you've said in mind for the future. How's that?"

Alice had no idea what to say to that—she couldn't figure out what Mike was insinuating. But she didn't think that she could say anything which would advance Boris's cause, so figured keeping her mouth shut would serve Boris the best. "OK."

"Gotta go, let me know what happens. This is quite exciting!" Mike rang off.

Alice started to put her phone into her pocket, still thinking about Boris. When the phone vibrated again, she didn't really look at the screen while answering, expecting it to be Mike with some other advice or direction which was nebulous and confusing. "Did you forget something?" she asked wearily.

"Uh... is this Alice?" asked the voice on the other end. It definitely wasn't Mike.

"Um. Yes, yes this is Alice."

"Hi, Alice, this is Scott. Victoria said that you wanted to talk to me?"

"Scooter?"

His smile was detectable through the phone. "Yeah. Scooter."

"Oh yes, yes. Um, can we talk face to face? I have some things I have to ask you. It's very important."

"Victoria mentioned that it very definitely wasn't to do with the current legal situation between your employer and myself."

"That's true."

"And you're presumably not able to tell me what this is about over the phone?"

"That's also true."

"OK, let's meet then. There's a Wetherspoon's called the Surrey Docks near Canada Water, I can meet you there at 10:00. Would that work for you?"

"I'd have to look at Google Maps to see how long that would take for me to get there."

"Are you at the office?"

"Near enough."

"You shouldn't have any trouble. It's a 40-minute bus ride or 30 minutes on the Jubilee."

"Awesome, I'm on my way now."

Wetherspoon's is a chain of pubs in England popular among students and the elderly—cheap drink and questionable food. As you would expect, the customers frequenting such watering holes on a weekday morning aren't the most salubrious.

A single elderly gentleman in a flat cap and liver spots sat in one corner nursing a pint while reading a newspaper, while two other rather unkempt individuals were arguing passionately with some sort of electronic trivia machine in the corner. Apart from the waitress and barman, the only other person south of fifty was a whippet-thin guy about Alice's age sitting in the corner watching her. She was surprised that he had a pint in front of him. He didn't get up as she approached but did shake her hand when she held it out.

"Nice to meet you, Scott," she said.

"Likewise," he responded. "Now, what's this all about?"

"I've come about the encryption work you've been doing."

He eyed her carefully. "The work which is currently the cause of a number of legal actions? That work?" He gave her a wry grin. "What about it?"

"Does it work?"

His grin changed to a frown in an instant. "What do you mean, 'does it work'? Does it work? Of course it works! Who would go to the trouble of suing me for something that doesn't work?"

"So can you tell me how it works?" she asked, leaning forward.

"Maybe you should tell me who you are and why you care so much? If you're not one of Thomas's lawyers, then who are you? What is your interest in my little side project?"

Alice was taken aback. These were all perfectly valid questions, but not ones she had thought to prepare an answer for. One thing that she knew was that spies certainly didn't admit to being spies, so the truth was totally out of the question. She watched him for a minute, trying to figure him out. He had a shaggy mop of dark hair which partly hid a youthful face that had shadows under its big brown eyes. "I'll be honest with you, I work for Richard Grant."

"I don't know who that is," responded Scott, taking a sip of his beer.

That threw Alice a little. She thought he would be impressed by her connection with such an entrepreneur. Surely someone with a side hustle would know Richard? She tried a different tack. "My employer has tasked me with finding out if the encryption you've been working on is legitimate."

"Why? So he can find out if it's worthwhile to sue me too? Let me guess, he leases Thomas his computers and he figures if I used one of those computers then that gives him a claim on my work? I'm sorry, try again. There's no benefit to me talking to you. At worst it undermines my defence in court."

"OK, look, I have my own reasons for asking. Unrelated to any legal conflict you're having."

Scott picked up a large paper menu which was on each of the tables. Alice knew that it was a list of various foodstuffs long on taste and short on nutrition which promised a lot for a low, low price. She knew that they were all pretty much the same throughout the chain and could almost guess every item and price from her student days. Scott made a show of selecting the wings and smiled up at her. "Look, I'm going to have some breakfast, but if you don't have a more compelling reason for me to talk to you, I'm afraid you've come all the way here to watch me eat some bad fried food and drink a beer which I suspect is a day or two from going off." He took note of the table number, marked on a circular medallion embedded in the wood of the table, and then headed up to the bar.

Alice could feel herself panicking. She had to think of some reason which would sound plausible but which would mean that Scott would be able to trust her with talking about his project. Maybe she could explain how she was on his side? He came back to the table but before he could speak, Alice jumped up and headed to the bar herself. She figured if Scooter was treating himself to breakfast then so could she. The waitress behind the bar looked up expectantly and Alice ordered the vegetarian breakfast plus a pint of lager. She asked for the table number and Alice gestured with her chin that it was for the same table. It took a minute to pour her beer and Alice took her first sip before returning to rejoin Scott, who looked a little surprised at her return.

"Look, it's like this," she started. "I don't care about your legal issues. That's not my concern—except to say that as a fellow coder, it sucks. But I am very interested from a technical point of view as to whether the encryption system works. And here's the thing—if you just talk to me about the technical nuts and bolts of your invention, none of that can help or hurt you in court, right? None of it is about when you did what. None of it is about what contracts were in force when you created any of the code. I don't care about that rubbish. I want to hear about the technical details of the system." She leaned back and took a draught of her beer. Disgusting.

Scott nodded slowly. "You're right. OK. What do you know about encryption?"

Alice sighed. Everyone wanted to know how much she knew about codes.

Scott smiled. "Relax, I won't mansplain it to you. You're a coder, did you say? Fine, if I go too fast, raise your left hand, if I'm going too slow, raise your right. I don't know what you know, so if I get too basic it's not because you're a girl, it's because I don't know how much you know, OK?"

Alice nodded, impatient to get going. "Fine—left explain more, right explain less."

Scott started his explanation. "OK, so the building block of life is DNA. It's a helix—a spiral staircase—and the steps are one of four types. Scientists don't call these A, B, C and D like normal folk would, no, they're named after their amino acid names so you end up with A, C, G and T. The spiral staircase is really, really long and you unzip it to just get the steps out, you end up with a really long string of letters. 'Mapping the genotype' consists of writing down that long list and because it's not an exact science, you may have to do it a few times to make sure there were no problems with the measuring."

"Thomas called it having to take multiple photos in case one part of one of them was blurry."

Scott's lips thinned at the mention of Thomas's name, but he nodded. "Yeah, that's about right. And so if you get that string of letters and remove the strings which are the same for everybody, what is left is what makes up Alice."

"And you can use that as a key for codes."

"Well... not really."

Alice looked up from her drink. "Huh?" she managed. Just then, their food arrived—Alice's breakfast and some sort of fried meat platter for Scott.

"So, what do you know about DNA?"

"Just what you've told me," replied Alice.

"Here's a question then. What about twins? Do twins have the same DNA?" Scott didn't wait for an answer. "And clones, do clones have the same DNA? And do you always have the same DNA? Does it ever change?"

Alice took a bite of vegetarian sausage. "Yes?" she tried.

Scott smiled, not unkindly. "The correct answers were 'yes', 'yes' and 'yes'. Twins and clones share the same DNA and DNA does change over time. Sometimes, therefore, some twins do have different DNA because they change at different rates. And if DNA changes, how can you use it as a key for a code? Surely the key to the code has to stay the same, otherwise you couldn't unlock something you encrypted years ago, right?"

"So you can't use the DNA as a key, after all?" tried Alice, feeling like she was on a roller coaster.

"About this time last year, I reached that same conclusion. Disheartening." Scott stripped a chicken wing of its flesh and added the bones to the little pile on the side of his plate. "But then I started looking at where the DNA changes occur. And when. And I started looking for patterns."

"Wait, hang on, are you a coder? This sounds like a lot of biology."

"Oh, didn't you know? I've got a Master's in Molecular Biology. I taught myself coding and wanted to get some practical experience so that I could do my own coding for my own project, so I took on the job with Thomas."

Alice raised her eyebrows. That was a surprise. "So what patterns did you discover?"

Scott shook his head. "I'm sorry, that's proprietary. Let's just say I eventually found the rhythm with which the changes to DNA can happen. And when I figured out what was driving those changes, I could code those changes. And when you can predict what a person's DNA will look like at a certain point in time, then you don't need to worry about the fact that it changes."

"And what about twins? And clones?"

"Clones are easy. If you can predict what a person's DNA will look like at any point during their life then having a person thirty years further along that journey than their clone means that you will know which you have depending on who has those thirty years of changes and who does not. Twins are even easier. You see, the DNA changes you can predict are not tied to the DNA itself so, for the prediction system, you are practically dealing with two totally different human beings. All those perfectly sound reservations about using DNA as an encryption key are gone." He smiled and leaned back, placing the last of the chicken bones on the pile and wiping his fingers on his napkin.

Alice thought the speech most compelling but had learned long ago that the code tended to be different from the marketing spiel. "So... how much of this is actually coded up?"

Scott washed down the last of the chicken with a mouthful of beer. "Oh, it's fully functioning. You would need a couple of days and about £5000 to sequence a person's genome, but my system takes a little longer because of that other part I mentioned. You need a few samples of living tissue, but that is easy enough to extract and about a week later you have it ready to go. Every year you update the system and... well, that's it. A 4MB encryption key that changes over time and is tied to your biological make-up. I've tentatively called it Magic, but the marketing people I was talking to before the legal action thought that they would be able to come up with something much better."

Alice had been eating while Scott talked but paused to wipe some of the grease off her face with a napkin. "And now tell me about the distributed messaging system."

Scott smiled. "That is even simpler. In fact, it's downright too simple."

Alice held up her right hand. "Get to the point," she said, winking.

"Fine. So, take fifty people who don't want anyone looking over their shoulder at what they're up to. Let's say three crime syndicates and two terrorist cells, each with ten people each. They know that intelligence agencies look at their call metadata. So not what the calls actually were or what was said, but rather the fact that Joe talked to Frank on this date, for this long. Data about the calls, not the calls themselves."

"Got it."

"So, if all the messages get repeated to all the fifty nodes, then there's no way that they can actually make any sense of the network traffic. You can't tell that Joe talked to Frank on this date for this long because, according to the traffic, he also talked to the other forty-eight people as well."

"That doesn't make sense," started Alice. "Because if Joe talked to Frank and the system connected the other phones to Frank at the same time, then they'd all go through to voicemail."

Scott smiled through his messy fringe back at her. "Conference Calls. Each time you call someone on the network, all the other people not already using their phones automatically join the same conference call."

Alice frowned. "So they hear things that they're not supposed to?"

Scott's smile got wider. He seemed to be enjoying himself. "No! That wouldn't be any good. No, the system reads a pair of random eBooks backwards and forwards for fake participants for the length of the call and then they disconnect. If you pick up your phone to make a real call it disconnects from the conference call and away you go. You need a large enough group of numbers to make sure there are enough fake participants to muddy the waters in case anyone is trying to keep tabs on you. If you only had three people involved, then it would be obvious who was really talking the second you interrupted the conference call to make a real call."

"Wow, you seem to have thought of everything!" said Alice.

Scott mock bowed. "Why, thank you, ma'am."

"So, do you have a demonstrable site? Something where you can see the whole thing working?"

Scott's smile dropped. "I had to take down the demo site because of the legal cases, and even then you need the tissue sample so there's a lot of setup involved. Why do you want a demo site?"

Alice smiled enigmatically. "I have an idea."

THE HOOK IS SET

The beer she had drunk was only partly soaked up by the vegetarian breakfast she'd eaten, so the late morning had a cheery glow as Alice made her way back to the office. She had a little time on the bus back to think about what to do next. She counted all the people who were interested in Scott's communication systems—there was Thomas who had promised Richard that it existed and that he owned it; there was Richard who represented The Handler's interest in it; and then there were the lawyers who shone the light of the law in deciding who should have it; and, finally, she realised she and Mike also had an interest in it. Alice wondered if as many people had been watching Isaac Newton getting hit by an apple and cheering him on to discover gravity. She sent Mike a text message stating that although she hadn't seen it, the code was apparently legit.

She arrived back in the office, smiled at Dolly on the way in, and headed towards Thomas's office. On the way there, she stuck her head into Victoria's office and thanked her for the connection. Thomas's door was open and he was behind his desk talking on the phone. He held up one finger as soon as he saw her and finished the conversation he was having. He looked up expectantly, the usual stupid grin on his face. She then realised that while some people had 'resting bitch face' where their neutral expression was one people misinterpreted as anger, annoyance or contempt, Thomas had the opposite. What to call that though? 'Resting nice face'? Alice realised that she was a little drunk and that Thomas was talking to her.

"Sorry, I zoned out there for a second. What were you saying?"

"I was just asking if you knew what you were going to tell Richard yet?"

"Ah, yeah, no, not yet."

"OK, so... what exactly can I do for you?"

Alice wasn't sure what she'd gone back to the office for, actually. "Uh... I'll get back to you on that one," she said, getting to her feet and heading back out past the front desk and back out into the fresh London air. Maybe she shouldn't have had that beer. She started walking, not really caring where her feet were taking her, just enjoying being outside. She crossed the river on London Bridge, enjoying the slightly emptier streets in the pre-lunch period. She passed Monument where the Great Fire had started and remembered climbing the stairs to the top. She'd gotten a certificate for that. She'd been stuck behind a larger man who had managed to get to the top and then had stood outside on the viewing deck for half an hour afterwards wheezing as if he was going to have a coronary. The views from there were mediocre but were certainly earned, which had made the climb worthwhile. The view from the shopping centre beside St Pauls was quite the opposite—accessed via a lift and with stunning views of both the cathedral and the surrounds, it was totally unearned.

The partially formed plan that she'd thought of over breakfast was starting to percolate and she sent Mike a text message asking if they could meet. By then, the final touches should have clicked into place and she ought to be in a position to present a fully formed suggestion. She would have to steer clear of Richard for a while and hope that Thomas would cover for her if Richard got in touch with him directly, but she was starting to see a way forward.

She wandered through the City—the bustling heartbeat of the financial district —skyscrapers looming overhead, looking out of place amongst the historical buildings. Far to the east, Alice knew that Canary Wharf was the satellite CBD built much more recently and looking more the part, with the surrounding buildings all being built in glass and steel. She'd reached Liverpool Street Station when her phone vibrated. She looked down and saw that Mike had replied. 'Can make lunch at my club or a pre-dinner drink. Let me know and I'll send the address'. She looked at her watch. Still time to get to his club before lunch. She replied accordingly and Google Mapped her route. Maybe she could get a cheeky vodka over lunch. This spy game was turning her into a lush!

The Club was everything she expected. Dark wood panelling. Portraits of men with the most serious mutton chops imaginable staring impassively from the walls. She walked up to the front counter and an impeccably dressed young lady looked up as she approached. The uniform seemed to be dark vest over white shirt with dark trousers. On closer inspection, the dark vest had a paisley pattern picked out in gold thread which looked very elegant. She asked for Mike by name and was led down a hall towards the dining room, the subdued clink of cutlery and glasses indicating that she was heading the right way. As they passed other rooms along the hallway, she glanced inside and saw lounges with high ceilings, comfortable armchairs and more old men than she would expect to see in a rest home. All well-dressed in suits and ties and either in quiet conversation or ignoring the world while reading large newspapers, amber liquid in tumblers on side tables.

The dining room shared the same high ceilings but instead of the dark wood and shadowy corners she'd spied in the lounges, this room was painted white and was well lit by a stylish chandelier in the middle of the room. The windows overlooked a square of green bordered by a thin line of trees, somehow out of place in the centre of the city—a secret haven surrounded by the Georgian and Victorian mansions. Mike was already at their table, standing to greet her before they were both seated and menus made available. A waiter—no vest, though the same white shirt and dark trousers—asked if he could get her a drink. She saw that Mike was drinking water, so asked for the same. She may need her wits about her and the buzz from the beer for breakfast was starting to wear off. She wondered about the men in the lounge, drinking hard liquor during the day. And Scott having beer for breakfast. While the men in the lounge were not exactly the best specimens, Scott had not seemed too badly affected by the diet. Maybe the beer in the morning represented his only carbs—he had seemed very slim.

The waiter returned with her water and asked if they knew what they would like to order. Mike ordered the nut loaf and looked expectantly over at Alice.

"I'll just have the side salad, please."

"Oh, don't worry about the bill, Alice. The chef here does a particularly good chicken chasseur—not too heavy at all."

"I... actually I had a rather large breakfast with Scott," she explained. "If I have anything more, I think I might pop."

Mike smiled, and the waiter bustled off. "I spent some time in New Zealand and they have a saying there from the Lord of the Rings movies - 'we've had first breakfast, yes, but what about second breakfast?'"

She smiled politely, adjusting her napkin in her lap.

"So, tell me what's on your mind."

She told him about Scott and his encryption program. Mike listened intently at first before extracting his phone from his jacket pocket. It folded out to double the original size and he pulled out a stylus and started writing on the screen. "Sorry, carry on," he said. She told him everything about the shortcomings of the system and Scott's efforts in addressing them. She then started on the distributed message system. When she got to the part about a network where all the phones were on all the same phone calls, Mike made a face and looked at the ceiling. She looked quizzically at him.

"The call patterns are some of the most valuable tools we have at the moment. There will be some upset people if this technology is widely adopted."

Alice shook her head at him. "It's not like it is a unique idea—anyone can make the system—Scott is probably just the first one to put it together."

Mike looked lost in thought. "Maybe we could get an injunction preventing him from going live with it. National interest and all that."

Alice felt a stab of panic at having to tell Scott that it was true that she had spoken to him unrelated to the current legal issues he was facing but, hey, here is another legal injunction, and this time the government would be the one on the other side. She could imagine that she might be off his Christmas card list after that.

"Sure, you could do that," she said. "Or we could use the systems as bait to get The Handler." She started on her salad. Mmmm, horseradish.

Mike's attention was back on her. "What do you mean by that?" he asked, his fork paused in mid-air.

Alice took another bite of salad. "It seems to me that we have an issue with getting The Handler back into the country where he can be arrested."

"Yes," stated Mike. His fork hadn't moved.

"And The Handler has shown some considerable interest in the encryption and message system which Scott has created."

Mike didn't say anything. He also didn't move his fork. He seemed to be willing Alice to continue without wanting to say anything.

"Luckily the encryption system is run off DNA. If we can persuade him that it requires an in-person sampling of his DNA, and maybe a couple of samplings over different days, then we can get him to come to the UK to perform that sampling. When he turns up for the DNA extraction, we arrest him."

Mike slowly ate the portion of food that had been suspended for so long in front of his mouth. He didn't say anything for a while. "There's a lot to like about that plan," he said eventually. "But there are some things that need ironing out. I assume that Scott's system doesn't actually need someone to be in the country for the sampling, does it? How do we persuade The Handler that it does? Why would Scott cave in on the legal situation? The Handler isn't a fool. If he gets told that he can have his toy all of a sudden on the condition that he comes to the UK—the one place where he is wanted for a multitude of crimes—he will be very suspicious. How do we put his mind at ease? And how do we know that he will actually show up? There are only two people in the country who have seen him well enough to recognise him if they saw him again."

Alice's interest was piqued. "Who are those two?"

Mike gave a wry smile. "One is me, the other a friend of mine. A long story. Anyway. What can you tell me about Scott? Will he play ball?"

It was Alice's turn to take her time in replying. "If you offered to buy out any tech entrepreneur before they released their product, what would you expect their response to be? They typically have heard of examples of undervaluing their own invention, or they value their ideas so highly that no amount of money would compensate them."

Mike smiled. "Good point—they all have a point to prove, don't they? Hmmm... Maybe we dangle the carrot of making the legal problems go away."

Alice frowned, feeling her face grow hot. "You said that you couldn't intercede for Boris, but you would for Scott?"

Mike was surprised by her anger. "Oh no! No, they're two totally different things. Look, for me to intercede for Boris, I would be interfering in a disciplinary procedure of the police force. Totally illegal, immoral and bad. And I don't have the power to intercede between The Handler's lawyers and Scott—that's a civil case. The most I could do is try to mess with procedural activities by the courts but that would again be stupid because it wouldn't get us anywhere. And would still be illegal, immoral and bad. No, I'm talking about telling Scott a little bit of the truth." He took a mouthful of water.

"I doubt Scott has the sort of money that would be required to mount a defence for all these court cases, right? And I imagine his time would be much better used on his programming project. All we have to do is let him know that should the person responsible for his legal pains come to the country for a DNA sample—which is not possible to do from afar, and he can't send a finger in a freezer box—then all of a sudden his legal issues will disappear and he will get his invention back."

Alice shook her head. "That will be a huge leap in trust. At least with the court case, he has a very slim chance of winning. This plan will be seen as a trick. He would have to give in with no guarantee of success. In fact, he's guaranteed to lose his invention. That's how he will see it."

"So we have to persuade him that the legal approach won't work. Talk to his lawyers. Talk to him. Find out what the lawyers say about his chances. About how much it will cost to defend. And then see if he'll take the bait. I'll get in touch with my guy at International Trade and see if the system qualifies for export controls. We might be able to block the transfer of intellectual control on the grounds that the ownership structure would constitute an attempt to evade export controls." Alice looked confused, which Mike misinterpreted as disbelief. "Look, it's worth a try."

Alice chased the last slice of cucumber around the plate, making sure it was well covered in the remnants of the dressing. "It sounds like I have to sell our friend Scott on our position."

Mike smiled. "You spend your life coding, you get really good at it, and then someone from the Home Office wants you to be a salesperson. You've done really well, Alice. You've got a nose for sniffing out the important facts. Stick with it—Scott is a technical person, you speak the same language, and you know what is at stake. You'll get him to our side. I believe in you."

Alice eyed him with a wry grin.

"What?" asked Mike.

Alice iterated through her fingers on one hand. "One, I was never a super expert at coding. Two, Richard is getting me to be a project manager, so the Home Office isn't the only one wanting me to change roles. Three, it seems every conversation ends with you believing in me. I'm not a mythical creature, Mike. But I get it. I'll talk to Scott. I'll get him on board."

Mike looked a little abashed but returned her smile. "That's all I can ask for, Alice."

Twenty minutes later, Alice had left Mike at the club and was wandering back towards the tube station. She had her phone in her hand and pulled off the main pavement to stand in the part next to the river. The lock screen showed that she'd missed calls from both Thomas and Richard, but she ignored those and found the call she'd had earlier that day with Scott. She hit Scott's number and waited.

"Hello?"

"Hi, Scott. Alice here from earlier today. I think I've found a way for you to get rid of your legal issues."

"What? How?"

"I think this conversation deserves an in-person discussion, don't you? Where can I meet you?"

"Back at the Docks?"

"I can be there in... call it an hour."

"I'll see you then."

The two men arguing with the quiz machine were gone, but there were more people in the pub when she walked back in. Most were a little rough around the edges, but the cavernous interior meant that the place felt empty enough for Alice to feel it was a good place for private conversation. Scott was just ordering a drink at the bar, so she joined him there.

"I meant to ask you if you normally had a beer with breakfast at ten in the morning," she said.

"Only since the letters from Thomas's lawyers. They've become more aggressive with that new firm he hired."

Alice ordered a half-pint of shandy to keep him company and they found a vacant booth.

"OK, tell me. How do I get the evil off my back?"

"Have you ever done Judo?"

Scott looked confused. "I have to fight them?"

Alice laughed. "No—judo is one of those martial arts where you use the opponent's strength against him. So, he lunges at you and you move in the same direction and give them a hip flip and they go flying. You use their momentum against them."

Scott wasn't following. "I don't follow."

Alice tried a different tack. "Do you have a lawyer?"

Scott looked wary. "Yes, I got a referral for an employment lawyer from a family friend."

"And what did they say about your case?"

A flash of anger crossed Scott's face. "They said that it would cost me £100,000 and that I would lose."

"Not the answer you were wanting, right?"

"No. I spent years studying, and then years considering the problem and then years figuring out the right way of making it work. Working for Thomas was my way of perfecting my coding abilities and now all that *time* and *effort* will be ripped out from under me."

"You're angry."

"You're damn right I'm angry! Thomas has no right to my code!"

"Let me paint you a picture. You're going to go home tonight. You will instruct your lawyer to fight the court case. You will go to court and you will lose. It will cost you £100,000. You will either hand over your code and equipment voluntarily or else you will be compelled to by the courts." Scott started to say something but she cut him off. "And if you try to destroy the code or otherwise make it so that Thomas can't have it, then the court will find you guilty of destroying Thomas's property and you may even go to court or become bankrupt."

Scott blinked away tears.

"Or you can do what I tell you..."

Scott took a sip of his beer, not making eye contact.

"You can do what I tell you, and we'll take out the guy behind the legal action. And when that happens the lawyers will get off your back, Thomas will back off, and you'll be able to do what you like with your code."

"What do you mean 'we'll take out the guy'? Who's 'we'? Isn't it Thomas behind this?"

Alice paused. "There's one guy in particular who is very interested in your code. We're very interested in him. Specifically getting him to come to the UK. If you help us do that then you get to keep your code. Simple."

Scott was looking at her through his fringe, his brown eyes wide. "Who *are* you, Alice?"

She ignored the question and took a sip of her drink. And waited. She'd made her pitch. She could see Scott turning over this new information and examining it from every angle in his head. It was fascinating watching a genius at work. Well, a genius that didn't know employment law. She almost expected him to say that he'd try his luck with the judicial system, probably out of some misplaced belief that he would somehow prevail even when his own lawyers had tried to explain how frail his case was.

She looked up and Scott was nodding slowly. "Tell me what I have to do," he said sadly.

"You have to ring Thomas and tell him to call off his lawyers. Tell him that you will play ball, that you will give him the code. That you will train people to use it, and you'll walk people through it. Basically, that you'll cooperate. But—and this is important—you must tell him that any DNA samples have to be taken in person. That it's not possible to send samples. Make up something to justify it. Decay of cell structures or needing multiple passes to ingest the data, something like that. Better still, tell him that it's a multiple-day process."

"What if the guy doesn't come to the UK? What if he sends someone else to test the system? Or if he still tries to send a finger or something despite my instructions?"

"If he sends someone else, we'll just have to use them as the test subject to prove it works and hope that our guy comes to have it set up straight afterwards."

"And if he doesn't? If he doesn't come into the country, then I don't get to keep my code, do I?"

Alice looked sad. "Look, you don't have any good choices. This is the least worst choice. You can contest the case and lose both your code and £100,000. Or you can try this. No guarantees, but at least there's a chance. And you can influence the outcome. Everyone agrees that the code is exciting, so you don't have to sell anyone on that. But you just have to come up with a vaguely scientific-sounding basis for why the extract ingestion has to happen in person and then you've got a chance. Don't overplay that by the way. The last thing you want to do is make them suspicious."

Scott rolled his eyes. "So persuade them that they need to come in person, but don't make it obvious that's what I'm doing."

"Stick to scientific reasons. They'll stop listening, trust me..."

Scott looked up sharply.

"...because Thomas is like that," Alice finished lamely.

"OK, I'll do it. I'll ring Thomas tomorrow and tell him."

"Ring him now. Tell him you're with me and that if he calls off the lawyers you'll cooperate. Don't tell him about the in-person ingestion just yet, wait until he brings you into the office."

Scott pulled out his phone and dialled.

She waited until she was on the way home before she looked at her messages. Richard had been checking up to see what progress she'd made, while Thomas was a little more desperate in tone, but pretty much the same message. The Overground ran in a tunnel under the Thames and when she came out the other side, she decided to make sure that Thomas knew who was responsible for Scott's change of mind. He was suitably impressed and effusive in praise of her accomplishment and she went home under a well-earned warm and fuzzy halo.

The next day she headed into the SpareSpace offices and Richard greeted her as she came in.

"Do you have an idea on the integration time yet?" he asked with a smile.

She took a stab in the dark. "Probably two or three months at the outside."

Richard looked delighted. "That's brilliant, well done. We'll get you to work on that immediately."

Alice smiled and sprang her trap. "Yes, I can get straight onto that," she said. "Just bear in mind that any DNA ingested into the system will have to be done in person."

Richard's smile barely faltered. "That's fine, that's fine. Hey, to say thank you properly, I've got two tickets to a gallery opening in Chelsea if you'd like to go. Free wine and canapes and pretentious art that's on loan from the US. Are you interested?"

"Definitely—when is it?"

"Wednesday night. I'll make sure that my PA gets you the tickets by the end of the day."

Alice spent the rest of the day weighing up who she should take with her. Her cousin Zoltan was a front runner, but it would be good to check in with Danica as well. She was such a crack up in situations like that—very social and outgoing which usually led to some fantastical adventures. The last time she'd gone out to a concert at the O2 they'd taken the ferry back and, as a result of fog and bad visibility, the ferry had made significant contact with one of the piers. They'd been well-liquored up from the concert and had elected to decamp at the pier rather than waiting an unknown length of time for the replacement ferry (Alice had been impressed with the fact that even the ferries could have replacement services). The trek home had included a stop-off in a truly dodgy pub, a kebab shop and meeting a visiting Spanish football team's supporters club. Danica had been in her element—great fun.

Zoltan would also enjoy the evening, but she was more in the mood for a less inhibited night rather than a serious appreciation of the art and an early tube home. So, the decision was pretty much made by the time the tickets showed up on her desk around afternoon teatime. She made sure she had the physical tickets in her hot little hand before sending Danica a text. The reply was almost instant. "Hell, yes!"

She got herself all dolled up, which entailed putting on a little black cocktail dress and heels. And then replacing the heels with something she could actually walk in. She recalled the effortless style of Victoria and wondered what she would recommend if Alice could use her as a fairy godmother. She'd love to be able to pull off such an effortlessly elegant look that Victoria used just for the office. She looked at herself in the mirror. The dress hung on her like a sack. She tried a belt to accentuate her slimness, but it just made her look like she was wearing a wristwatch around her waist. She took the dress off and put on a pair of black dress pants and a white T-shirt. That felt more like her, but it was a little less dressy than an art gallery seemed to require. And she wanted to make sure that there was no way she could be mistaken for any staff circulating with trays of wine. She looked through her clothes, interlopers in Zoltan's closet, but there wasn't anything there that really appealed. Maybe there was something in Zoltan's closet which he wouldn't mind if she borrowed? She started flicking through his clothes. And there it was—the perfect leather jacket. She tried it on and was surprised that she fit it so well. It must have been tiny on Zoltan. Sure, he wasn't the largest of men, but she was very slim, so she'd expected it to be boxier on her frame. She flicked Zoltan a quick text telling him that she'd possibly be home late and not to wait up and asking if it was ok for her to borrow the jacket. He responded pretty quickly stating that he didn't know about any leather jacket, so it would be fine if she borrowed it. She filtered the essentials from her purse and put them into the inside pocket of the jacket and grabbed her keys as she left the apartment.

She met Danica at the station near the gallery and she whistled as she took in what she was wearing. Alice had found a pair of sunglasses in the pocket of the jacket and was rocking the bad-girl model look reminiscent of the 90s. Danica on the other hand was playing to her strengths with a figure-hugging little black dress.

"We look like a movie star power couple," observed Danica, checking their reflections out in a convenient window before realising the patrons of the restaurant behind the window were getting a good show. Blowing the patrons kisses, they walked arm in arm towards the gallery, Alice clutching the ticket like one of Willy Wonka's golden tickets.

The gallery was a stark white space populated by a smattering of waitstaff scurrying amongst a sparse crowd of patrons. A string quartet was playing vaguely familiar music in the corner, and the cavernous venue seemed to overwhelm the number of installations. Alice looked at her watch. They were bang on time, so maybe other people would be arriving more fashionably late. Danica read her mind and stage-whispered, "More food and wine for us!", snagging two glasses of champagne from a passing waiter. They set off around the installations, fully intending on giving them a chance but dissolving into hysterics at the pretentiousness of some of them.

One, in particular, stood out. A corner of the gallery had been given an extra wall to make it look and feel like a small room or hallway. For some reason, the artist had scattered newspapers and magazines on the floor and put up posters on the walls. In the centre of the room, sitting on top of the carpet of paper stood a low stool on three legs. Danica peered into it and turned to Alice. "That looks like my brother's room from when we were teenagers. I half expect to be able to see his stash of porno mags in the corner."

"What does the stool mean?" Alice wondered aloud.

"What does any of it mean?" asked someone beside her in an American accent.

Alice's face fell and she cringed. "You're the artist, aren't you?" she asked, as she turned to see the speaker.

He was average height and somewhere in his late thirties, she thought. Average build, closely cropped beard with just a fleck of grey, not particularly handsome, but pleasant looking. He was smiling. "No, but I am the one who brought the exhibition to the country. You're lucky, with such a low turnout there was a high percentage chance of being overheard by the artist if he was here. I'm Hunter, by the way. Hunter Garrison."

She took his hand briefly. "Alice, and this is my friend Danica."

Danica giggled. "I was sure that you were going to say that your name was Hunter Gatherer."

Hunter rolled his eyes. "Don't get me started. My school days were *not* fun. Are you enjoying the exhibition?"

Alice watched him over her wine glass as Danica purred. "Some of the exhibits are a little..."

"...less obvious?" prompted Alice.

"...obtuse?" tried Hunter.

"...weird," finished Danica.

Hunter looked around. Seeing that they were almost alone, he gestured towards the installation on the other side of the room. There was no one around it and they strolled across, Alice and Danica looking at each other curiously.

"This is my favourite installation," Hunter explained, pointing. It was... intriguing, to say the least. Twelve poles, each about a fist in diameter rose from the floor to a fake ceiling ten feet high. Skewered by the poles were hundreds of hard-backed books, their pages in some cases jaggedly protruding from the covers and their alignment randomly distributed around the pole so that the spines seemed to circle the poles until they reached the ceiling. Hunter beckoned them over and they each stepped past the velvet rope which partitioned off the installation from the rest of the gallery.

"The best view is actually from inside looking out," said Hunter, moving to the back of the mini pantheon.

Alice paused to read some of the titles of the books, noting with interest that they were a mixture of contemporary and classic literature, all with the dust covers ripped off or missing and little in terms of rhyme or reason in their arrangement. She joined the others at the back, and Hunter showed them that the ceiling was painted white, but had an eagle etched into it with gold and electric blue paint, the fine lines barely visible until Hunter got out his phone and shone his torch app on the ceiling which reflected and illuminated the figure. She was worried that security might show up and throw them out and so looked out at the gallery beyond to see everyone ignoring them except for one of the waiters, who seemed quite concerned until he made eye contact with Alice and bustled off to distribute glasses of wine. Alice thought nothing of it except that this particular waiter didn't seem like the others. He was a little older than the other waiters, and, if Alice was honest with herself, he wasn't as good looking either. All the others seemed to be straight out of a fashion magazine—stick thin and very well maintained. They didn't so much walk around the gallery but floated. He, on the other hand, seemed like he needed a good meal and a good night's sleep. And he definitely did not float—rather, he lurched from patron to patron. Alice returned her attention to the conversation going on inside.

"It's not much fun travelling from country to country with the exhibition, but it does mean that I can see a bit of the sights before I supervise the assembly of the installations. We usually have a day or so to set up, then a week of exhibiting, followed by a pack down and then it's off to the next place. A week at a time and we're about two-thirds of our way around the globe."

Danica tapped him playfully in disbelief. "No way—you travel around the world for a year babysitting all this, and you do maybe two or three days of actual 'work' work each week? Where have you been?"

Hunter grinned, quite bemused by her reaction. "Well, we started in the States, obviously, heading from the West Coast to the East. Then up to Canada and back to the Pacific, leaving from Vancouver. Over the Pacific to Japan, and then through China into Russia and then on into Europe. We're billing it as the Peace Tour and after Europe we head down through the Middle East, through India and Southeast Asia to Australia and maybe New Zealand before heading back over the Pacific to LA."

"Wow," exclaimed Danica. "That must cost a fortune! Who pays for all of that?"

"Lots of governmental agencies and a few wealthy benefactors. The artist is able to sell each piece for millions, so this is pretty much an advertisement for the auction at the end of it."

"Oh, man, I want your job," said Danica. "How did you get this cushy job? Talk about lucky!"

Hunter's grin never reached his eyes. "Well, first I did Art History at UCLA and then did my Masters at Yale. I got 'lucky', as you call it, and did an unpaid internship at MoMa in New York and then managed to get work at a couple of private galleries. Sandwiched in there was a few years working at the auctions for Sotheby's. Finally, the artist himself decided he would trust me with these beauties. Funny, it never really felt like luck."

Alice watched him carefully. "New York is quite expensive, how did you manage to eat while not getting paid?"

Hunter's eyes sparkled as the rancour left him. "Now that *was* lucky—I stayed with a family friend."

Alice grinned back. "Staying with family friends is definitely the way to go!"

"Now that I've shown you the secret eagle, we should probably join the rest of the patrons before they decide that they can all come in."

Danica led Hunter away with some involved question and with hardly a backward glance the two of them slowly left the pantheon. Alice meandered behind but paused as she noticed two fluffy-tailed bookmarks sticking out of one of the books. She frowned and bent closer. Surely there was some symbolism here—who had the artist picked out as warranting two bookmarks? What great hidden meaning could there be—this book chosen amongst hundreds of others? She noted the title and author and her frown increased. *Pet Sematary* by Stephen King? What did *that* mean? She was still puzzling that as she left the installation and Hunter made a great show of reattaching the velvet rope behind them.

"Are the exhibits very valuable?" she asked.

Hunter nodded as he considered how to answer the question. "I know what you mean. How can they command such a high price if they are just paper and metal and paint? So, the answer is both yes and no. There's nothing intrinsically valuable with any of them—this is not a diamond-encrusted skull, this is not a gold plated shark cut in half and immersed in formaldehyde. And yet by the end of the tour, all of them will sell for multiple millions of dollars. Some even into the tens of millions."

Alice indicated the books behind them. "And the books?"

"Just books." Hunter grimaced. "Occasionally we'll have an issue with the installation and wreck one of the books so we'll just go and buy a replacement from a second-hand bookshop. Don't tell anyone," he stage whispered.

They all laughed.

Hunter looked around the auditorium. "Look, I have to mingle just in case someone here ends up being excruciatingly rich, or the representative of someone who is excruciatingly rich, but it was lovely talking to you both and I hope I bump into you later on in the evening." With a slight bow, he headed off across the gallery towards a couple who were examining one of the installations in silence, their heads cocked at exactly the same angle and their glasses held in exactly the same pose. Almost synchronised.

Danica and Alice did a circuit of the installations, trying to fathom what each one meant and resorting to reading the accompanying boards of information when they could not discern what was going on. Which was actually for all of them. It was impossible for them not to get a little giggly— the alcohol and the ludicrousness of the art combined—but they were discreet about their humour. The sparseness of attendance certainly helped.

Eventually, they happened to be at the same installation as someone else and watched the couple that Hunter had abandoned them for as they peered intensely at the digital display. The section of the wall was made up of about thirty large monitors with very thin bevels so that they operated like one large screen. On the left-hand side of the super screen was an animation of a farmer at work, a view of him in the field taken from a top-down view and at altitude, like an eagle might see. On the right-hand side of the screen was a map of countries with their borders changing over time. A little star in the middle of the map indicated the village where the man on the left lived. Across the top of the screen a date flicked through history very quickly, and descriptions of events flashed up beside it. Some of the events related to the maps with the borders constantly shifting—invasions, peace treaties, that sort of thing. Some of them related to the personal life of the man on the left-hand side—births, deaths, marriages. Periodically as they watched, the man on the left would disappear to be replaced by a woman or a man who was the child of the previous central character, and then they too would work in the field or in the village, performing the jobs dictated by the society of the time. They watched fascinated for a few minutes and then the border whiplashed across the map, flicking through the star in the middle and the view on the left was filled with soldiers and the person in the middle—Alice couldn't tell at this stage whether it had been a man or a woman—was now lying on the ground in the middle of the town.

Then the whole thing reset and started all over again, the day-to-day activities of the peasants totally ignoring the historical changes until they bulldozed through their lives, snuffing them out.

The woman of the couple nodded slowly as it started to repeat, turning to her partner who had been quite affected by the exhibit. "Very moving—very powerful, isn't it?"

"Yes, quite," he replied, snuffling into a handkerchief. They wandered off, deep in conversation.

Danica looked over at Alice, suddenly serious. "I think I understood that one," she said. "How about another drink?" she asked, and they headed back towards the bar. By now there were a few more people wandering around, the string quartet was still playing through the PA system and the background hubbub had become a notch or two louder. There was something familiar about what the string quartet was playing, but Alice could not quite put her finger on it. They snaffled some finger food from a passing waiter, the waiter's route adjusting as they reached for the food so that he pirouetted to a halt in front of them with the tray descending elegantly from head height to right in front of them. Alice thought she detected a twinkle of a smile from the waiter as he paused for them to help themselves and then headed back into the crowd, swaying in time to the music.

"Metallica!" Alice said suddenly. "And System of a Down!"

Danica looked over at her quizzically.

"The quartet. They're playing metal."

"Oh, ok. Mmmm! These are delicious!"

They grabbed a couple of glasses of champagne and some more hors d'oeuvres, impressed with the tastiness of the bite-sized morsels. Danica got chatting with a couple standing nearby, one of whom turned out to be a semi-famous actor who Alice had vaguely heard about—she'd apparently been in Australia when the show he'd been in had enjoyed its moment of fame. They had a good ten-minute conversation that roamed widely and was punctuated by periodic visits from their favourite waiter who, Alice noticed, actually grooved through the crowd. He must be a dancer, she decided. Danica noticed her watching the waiter depart after delivering the latest tasty treats and gave her a grin.

A half-hour and another glass of wine later, Alice was feeling nicely buzzed. When the waiter came around again, she noticed the less than dextrous waiter taking a tray of empty wine glasses back to the bar. She beckoned the favourite waiter closer and he swung down with the tray as usual. As she helped herself to a caramelized onion tart, she nodded towards the other waiter and frowned.

"What's his story?" she asked.

The waiter looked over to where she was indicating and rolled his eyes. "Replacement," was all he said before sashaying away. As the night was progressing, the crowd was growing, the wine was flowing and the waiter was getting more and more groovy. The more fluid everyone else got, the less fluid the uncoordinated waiter's movements were becoming. He didn't drop any drinks or anything obvious like that, but he moved as if he was being pulled in different directions. When the other waiters moved past with a tray of wine, there was no sound from the tray. When the uncoordinated one walked by all the glasses clinked, whether they were full or empty. Alice was a little drunk and started to think of him uncharitably as Lurch.

The great thing about Danica was that, given a social occasion and a few drinks, she opened doors and would speak to anyone, which nine times out of ten led to a good conversation. People really enjoyed talking with her and it was easy to coast along in her wake—the perfect spot for a wallflower like Alice. And that's how the night went—a blur of conversation, laughter, witty banter and fleeting connections. The exhibition had started off as the focus of the evening, but as the crowd grew and more and more wine was drunk, the conversations turned inwards and the good looking and semi-famous found more important things to talk about. Alice noticed Hunter periodically through the night, pressing the flesh, being very sociable and effervescent, but the opportunity to refresh their acquaintance never presented itself.

Eventually, the night came to a close, with the main lights coming back up and the music stopping. Hunter had found a microphone and stood on the stage as the musicians were putting their instruments away, and eventually a hush fell on the crowd.

"Thank you all for coming, I hope you enjoyed yourselves. Thank you to the venue for the outstanding food and drink and thank you to the lovely Four Roses String Quartet for the great music."

Alice and Danica had found themselves talking to a couple outside the pantheon exhibit and Alice couldn't help but notice that Lurch had stepped over the velvet rope and had entered the exhibit, returning seconds later carrying an empty wine glass in front of him as if he had retrieved it from inside the exhibit. The only flaw in that plan was that Alice had seen him carrying it in with him.

Hunter finished his speech, and the crowd started to disperse. Alice knew that Hunter had said that there was nothing intrinsically valuable in the exhibit so she didn't know why Lurch would have gone inside. She shrugged to herself and turned her attention to how she was going to get home. Danica lived in a different direction, so they compromised, sharing a cab to London Bridge, where it dropped Danica off for the train home, before the taxi driver was instructed to head back across the river and deposit Alice outside Zoltan's apartment. A good night out.

UNCLE REGGIE

She woke with the sun shining into the apartment's floor-to-ceiling window. It was actually reflecting from the windows of the building across the road, but the effect was the same—a sharp stabbing pain piercing through her eyeballs and into her brain. She managed to stand up without throwing up, but everything was unsteady. Zoltan handed her a large mug of steaming coffee.

"I've got to go to work, but you look terrible. Is that the jacket? Doesn't look familiar." He paused, looking at her with concern. "Are you going to be alright?"

She took a sip of the coffee. Intensely focusing on the action of moving the mug to her lips somehow blocked out the pain momentarily, for which she was grateful. It did mean that she missed what Zoltan just said though. "Huh?" she managed.

Zoltan rolled his eyes. "I should wait until you're 100% but we should probably talk about the living arrangements. I was happy to let you stay while you were getting settled, but you've had your job for a little while now, so it might be time to start thinking about getting your own flat."

Alice started to nod in agreement but that allowed her brain to remember it didn't like her and waves of nausea racked her body. She sat on the stool at the breakfast bar, groaning a little. "Sure, uh, tonight?"

Zoltan patted her in a brotherly fashion on the shoulder. "Maybe you should call in sick. You do really look terrible. We'll chat when I get home."

She rang the office and made her apologies, feeling both sorry for herself and a little guilty that her self-inflicted ailment had led to her missing a day's work. In an attempt to justify it to herself, she thought about getting Scott to agree to drop the legal challenges, and how she had been super productive in getting the desired results. She couldn't shake her programmers' criterion for productivity though—not how many lines of code, but the amount of fully tested and documented functionality added to the code base. How did salespeople and managers judge their productivity without being able to see the fruits of their labour? Thinking of Scott, she settled down on the couch and dialled his number.

"Hullo, Alice. I did what you asked. When do I get my code back?"

"Slow down, Scott. I just rang to say thanks for doing the right thing and to let you know it will take a little time for everything to shake out how we want it to. But, most importantly, you should let me know when they want an example of your code."

There was silence on the other end of the phone, so Alice continued.

"We've dropped the hints that any use of the code will require an in-person visit, so we really need to get things set up in preparation for that once it happens."

Scott started to say something, probably to protest or to say that he couldn't do it, so Alice continued.

"Look, the pace of when you get your code back isn't actually in our hands. We are now in a reactive state—we need to prepare and move as soon as they start talking in any way about a demonstration. Do you understand?"

"Yes, as I've been trying to explain, Thomas has already been in touch and I need to show it working to one of his colleagues, so we are taking a sample at his airport hotel out near Heathrow tomorrow."

Alice felt numb. "Scott," she stammered. "Could you tell me a bit more about that?"

Scott obviously didn't have any concept of how his statement had impacted Alice. "Sure. Soon after I got off the phone with Thomas to tell him that I was willing to settle, maybe a couple of hours after that, I got a phone call from the lawyers saying that they were withdrawing the claims against me. Then I got another call from Thomas wanting to set up a demonstration of the code working. I remembered what you said about telling people it had to be in person, which seemed to be news to him. He said he'd ring me back and then first thing this morning he wanted to set up the appointment, telling me that I should get all the equipment that I needed and ready to go this afternoon. And that I should head out to Heathrow and he'd be able to tell me the hotel and the room number when I was there. He wouldn't tell me who I'd be taking the sample from, so I want you to come to help out."

Alice knew she had to talk to Mike. Now. "Uh... Scott, I have to talk to someone, but listen to me. I need for you to stay where I can get in touch with you. Don't go anywhere. Don't talk to anyone on the phone. Just sit down somewhere and... just wait for me to call you back." She hung up.

She dialled Mike but it went straight to voicemail. She tried again and again a perky voice invited her to leave a message after the beep. She was a little panicked and tried to explain what was going on, but it came out in a stumbling rush of words devoid of coherence. She tried to re-record the message but accidentally saved it. Sighing, she rang back a third time and took a breath to calm herself before laying out the facts and imploring him to get in touch with her so she could let Scott know what the plan was.

She weighed up just sitting and staring at the phone, but she was so out of it she thought she might fall asleep and decided to try and wake herself up with a shower. She propped the phone up on the shelf above the sink so she could see the screen from inside the shower cubicle and ran the water. She thought it would be best to try and become more human before she was required to apply any intellectual effort. The hot water helped. She emerged, radiantly pink and glowing and able to think relatively clearly at last.

As she dressed, the phone rang and she tripped on the towel in her attempt to answer it. Panting a little, she heard Mike's voice, excitement evident in his tone, volume and pace.

"Great news Alice, but we have to move quickly. Can you get Scott out to Heathrow with all the equipment that he needs? If you can get him out there, then we can take it from there. I'll pull in some favours—talk about short notice! Will you have any problems with that side of things? Is he on board? Will he be able to do the sample extraction?"

It was a little bit too much, too soon for Alice. "Uh... slow down, Mike. I'll see if he can get out there. Do we go now? We don't know the hotel or room number or anything."

"I'll get a situation room set up and let you know where that is. That might take a couple of hours."

"OK, so we'll wait until we hear from you then?"

"No, collect Scott and get him out to Heathrow. It'll take you that long to get out there. By that stage, I should have some directions on where to go. Game time!"

Alice rang Scott to let him know that he should head out to Heathrow immediately. "Hi Scott, how soon can you get out to Heathrow with all the equipment you'll need?"

"Uh... call it ninety minutes. Should I meet you on the way?"

"That sounds great—I'll meet you at Paddington."

"Paddington? I'm not going through Paddington."

"Well, how are you going to catch the Express if you don't go to Paddington?"

"I'm not—I'm catching the Piccadilly line. I can meet you at Green Park if you like—that's where I'll change lines."

Alice frowned. "Why are you taking the underground out to the airport? That will take ages."

"Yeah, but it's cheaper."

"Oh, for Christ's sake, I'll pay. Can you please just get out to Heathrow as soon as you can? Please, it is important."

"Fine. I'll meet you at Paddington in... call it an hour."

"Good." Had she been too hard on him? "Thanks for this, Scott. This is when you get your code back."

"OK, thanks. I'll see you in Paddington."

"Cool, see you soon."

She hung up and got dressed. Rather than move all her belongings from the pockets of the leather jacket she'd worn the night before into her handbag, she threw it on over her normal uniform of jeans and shirt. She slipped on some trainers to complete the look and headed out of the apartment at a trot.

She was famished by the time she reached Paddington and grabbed a Cornish pasty to eat while waiting for Scott to show up. She didn't realise how dehydrated she was until she drank the sweet orange fizzy drink she got as part of the combo. She watched the steady progression of tourists, business people and families wrangling children and suitcases from all corners of the station towards the Heathrow Express. After she'd finished the pasty and the drink, she deposited the wrapper and bottle into the rubbish bin and bought two return tickets for the Express. Just after she'd collected the tickets from the machine her phone buzzed with a text from Scott asking where she was. She eventually tracked him down—he had arrived from the Circle line, so was on the other side of the station and would therefore use a different gate to get to the train. She passed through the barriers and walked past the Express and up the exit ramp to the other gate where Scott was waiting and handed him his ticket so that he could come through. He was carrying a holdall and seemed a little skittish.

"You look terrible," he told her once he was through the barriers.

"Never tell a woman she looks terrible," Alice retorted. "Let's go," she said and led the way down the ramp to the train which was waiting on the platform. They settled into their seats and not long after the train pulled out. Alice wasn't in the mood for a lot of chatter and although Scott's nervousness made her feel like she should be trying to put him at ease, she was still feeling the effects of the previous night's drinking, so stared out the window at the cityscapes.

They arrived at the airport and left the station, heading the ramps to the passages leading to Terminals 2 and 3. They paused at the T intersection wondering which one to go to, before Alice pulled out her phone and, seeing no indication from Mike, shrugged and elected to head towards Terminal 2. By the time they had emerged from the underground tunnels into the antiseptic light of the arrivals level, Mike had sent an address via text message, so they detoured to the taxi rank and read out the address to the driver. He sighed and told them to get in.

They soon found out why he had sighed. After leaving the concrete maze of the terminals in the centre of the airport, they departed the airport proper via a tunnel that went under the runways, poking out the other side at a roundabout featuring a jet airplane in the centre of it. A quick left turn later they went maybe five minutes up the road before crossing to the other side of the dual carriageway and they were there, outside a hotel within spitting distance of the airport.

It must be the closest hotel to the airport without being actually on the airport, thought Alice to herself before heading to reception with Scott. They rushed through the lounge and bar, looking for Mike before Alice noticed that the address of the hotel was subtly different from the one Mike had sent through—the postcode was exactly the same, but the address was different. She went up to reception and showed them the address, and they pointed her to the side street beside the hotel which led to an industrial complex behind the hotel. A huge coolstore was the primary warehouse at the end of the lane, but it also had a police station just beyond the vehicle checkpoint. The pedestrian footpath didn't have any security checks on it, and the address on the wall of the station matched perfectly with that on Alice's phone, so they headed inside.

She asked the policeman on the counter for Mike Reid and he got them to sit in the waiting area and disappeared into the bowels of the station, reappearing a few minutes later with Mike in tow. He ushered them into a training room that had been repurposed as a situation room. A large-scale map of the airport had been put up on one wall, a long list of the hotel names joined to pushpins identifying their location by pieces of string.

Mike introduced himself to Scott. "Thank you so much for doing this. I've been waiting three years for this day and I'm very excited."

Scott looked confused. "Three years?"

Mike smiled. "You recall three years ago there was that little insurrection? A week and a half period where some louts decided to try and overthrow the government by executing a bunch of the rich?"

Scott nodded.

"Well, we think that this guy is the one responsible for that whole thing. We are gathering a team that will go in and arrest the suspect once we get a positive ID, so you're going to be in good hands."

Alice frowned at the way Mike had said that. "Won't you be there?" she asked.

Mike looked pissed off. "No... it's been decided that with my public profile, I am not to be involved with the identification of the suspect. Because we don't know which hotel we'll be in, we can't set up surveillance ahead of time and, anyway, to be 100% sure we really need to have an eyewitness confirm the identification."

"But if you're the only person who saw this guy back then how are you going to be an eyewitness now in person if you're not allowed to be involved?"

"There was one other person who we can trust to positively identify The Handler."

Just then an older man entered the room. He wasn't retirement age, but he was certainly approaching it. He was taller than average with a bald head and a thick moustache. He looked uncertainly around the room before seeing Mike and heading over and shaking his hand.

"Mike! Great to see you again! Meredith says to say hello. So, what's all this about?" He had an accent, but Alice couldn't tell if he was from Australia or New Zealand. Definitely not from Sydney though.

"Reggie, glad you could make it. Tell her that I said hi. We need you to make a positive ID on The Handler. Do you remember what he looked like from three years ago?"

"Sure, floppy hair, motorcycle jacket. What's not to remember? Do you have him in a holding cell? Or do you have some photos? Oh hullo, I'm Reggie." He reached over and shook hands with Alice and Scott.

"So, here's the plan Reggie. We'll get a phone call soon with the name of a hotel nearby and a hotel room number. There will be a guy waiting for us in that room who may or may not be The Handler. Scott here will go into the room with you and if it's The Handler you'll signal us, we'll come in and arrest him. Any questions?"

Scott piped up. "If I'm going in, Alice is going in. She got me into this, so she has to be there. Besides, I can get away with having a nurse to help me, but who is this guy?"

"If she can be a nurse, I could be a doctor, I guess," Reggie said, oblivious to the tension rising in the room.

"Out of the question, it's too dangerous. Alice is not needed in the room, so she won't be in there."

"But she is needed there, because if she's not there, then I won't be in there either. Nobody said that there would be danger."

Alice leaned close to Scott and whispered. "What's going on? Why are you putting your code at risk? This is where you get it back. Why are you fighting this?"

Scott breathed out heavily. "If you're there then I will get my code back, but if you're not there, what guarantee do I have?"

Alice shook her head. "That makes no sense. But hey, how about I wait in the lounge area of whichever hotel we're at? Will that be close enough for you to be happy..." she gestured towards Scott, "... and far enough away for you to be happy?" she asked, the last addressed to Mike.

The two men weighed up their positions silently before begrudgingly nodding. Reggie chose that moment to pipe up. "Right, the room will be too dangerous for Alice, but OK for me and this young man. Got it."

Mike smiled at Scott, Alice not sure whether it was genuine or not. "So all we have to do now is wait for the phone call."

One loose thread was bothering Alice. "What if it's not the guy you're looking for?"

Mike looked over at Reggie. "If you think it's not him, or if you're not sure, then you have to let us know so we can call off the backup squad. If that happens, then we will finish taking the samples and leave. Scott will run his tests and then we will regroup and think about what we can do. We've got a team waiting who can follow him as he leaves and we've got a team in each of the terminals ready to leave on whichever flight he's departing on."

Reggie nodded. "So how do I communicate with you?"

"We'll give you two cell phones, one for the 'yes it's him' call and one for the 'no it's not him' call. Just switch the phone on that aligns to whether you think it's him or not. We'll be monitoring the signal and know which one it is and either send the team in or pull back."

"That makes sense," grinned Reggie.

The waiting was unbearable, but eventually they were put out of their misery by the shrill cheesy ringtone coming from Scott's phone. Some pop hit from last year. He looked embarrassed as he answered it.

"Hullo, Thomas. Where is he? ... ok... cool, room 362, got it. .... I don't know, maybe an hour? OK, I'm on my way now. ... No, I've got a doctor friend of mine to help me. I don't want to screw up the sample collection and this is the first time I've done it outside the lab, so I'm very worried about getting things wrong. It would be so much easier if we could have done this in my lab, you know. ....ok. ..... Ok, cool, thanks, Thomas. Bye."

Scott walked over to the map on the wall, pointing to one of the hotels very near to where they were standing. "Room 362," he said needlessly.

Mike came over and put his hands on Scott's shoulders, looking him in the eye. "Remember this—you are needed alive. There is no reason for them to suspect anything. All you have to do is to take the samples and make sure that Reggie gets the chance to get a good look at the guy in the room. That shouldn't be hard. You do all the sample stuff and Reggie will waffle around, maybe washing things or putting things in the fridge, that sort of thing. And when you're finished, Reggie will do the phone thing. You'll be gone if we have to go in and you'll be gone if we have to follow him. Either way, you're going to be safe. Just do your thing, ok?"

Scott nodded, his floppy fringe and big brown eyes making him look very young indeed. "I'll be ok."

"And Alice will be in the foyer, waiting for you. You'll be fine. Now you know where you're going?" He nodded again and picked up his bag. The three of them made their way out of the station and onto the main road for the short walk to the hotel in question. Alice walked in with Scott and Reggie and then found a seat in the lounge area and sat down where she could see the reception area, the lifts and the hallways heading into the hotel. Reception was dealing with a knot of aircrew with their attendant wheelie cabin luggage, and she watched as Reggie and Scott called the lifts and then headed to the 3rd floor.

Now all she had to do was wait.

As she was waiting, one of the pilots came over and sat down opposite her. He didn't have any luggage but was carrying a tumbler of scotch in one hand and a magazine in the other. She smiled politely at him and he smiled back. He seemed nice enough, though he hadn't taken his hat off inside which seemed rude. At least he didn't have those ridiculous mirrored aviator glasses she'd seen in the movies. They were always overkill.

"Are you waiting for someone?" he asked. His accent was refined English. She nodded. "Me too," he said. His eyes narrowed. "Hey, didn't I see you at the gallery last night? At the art exhibition?"

She smiled slowly. He wasn't Lurch or any of the elegant waiters, so she guessed he must be one of the other guests. "And I'm still feeling the after-effects of it today, unfortunately."

"Do you believe in coincidences? Because I don't really. I saw you at the exhibition where someone stole a million pounds from me. And then here you are again, exactly where I am. Seems a little too coincidental, don't you think?"

Alice frowned. "I'm sorry someone stole your money, but I had nothing to do with it. Wait, how was there a million pounds at the exhibition? Was it in bullion? Or in cash?"

The pilot looked bored. "The problem when you live away from home is moving money to where it needs to be, to pay for things you need to buy. It's a curse of the job really, being away from home so much. So you learn ways that are harder to track, harder to block. You could move cash, but there are limits to how much cash you can use in transactions before it raises eyebrows, especially with lawyers. Turn up to pay them with a bag full of money and you're going to get some questions. And bullion is heavy and really easy to detect, so that's out too."

Alice wasn't following. "So what do you use? Gift cards?"

The pilot was now amused. "That's certainly what some people use, but again, really hard to pay the lawyer with gift cards. No, what people like myself use is e-currency. Bitcoin. That kind of thing. And the beauty of that is that you can send people the money with two pieces of paper. One, an account number—actually a wallet identifier. Useless by itself, but when you add the second piece of paper with a key on it—like a password but really long, then boom, you have access to a large amount of money which can't be traced and can pay any bill you might have. So nobody tracking your internet activity or your cell phone activity could possibly notice that you have paid someone or have a financial relationship with them. It's perfect. Unless someone takes the pieces of paper from an exhibit before your man can retrieve them. Somehow they knew exactly which exhibit they were in.

And exactly which book they were in. And then for reasons which really do escape me, they turn up the following day, protesting that they're hungover to rub it in my face, like stealing a million pounds from me was some sort of drunken jape. Stealing from a criminal can't possibly be a crime, right?"

Alice blinked. The pilot... was he The Handler? "Oh, fuck."

AN ARREST

"So you can see why I may be a little miffed, can't you?" continued The Handler. "And why I might take exceptional steps to exact a particularly painful revenge?"

Alice glanced around. There was nobody here that she knew. All the other people in the lounge area were too far away to catch their eye and the reception area had coped with the other aircrew. There was no sign of Scott or Reggie. She was on her own, but there was no reason why she couldn't just get up and leave, was there?

"I don't like being blamed for something that I didn't do. I didn't steal any money from you."

He stroked his chin, considering her. "I'm almost inclined to believe you. But the thing about animals when you corner them and death is imminent is that they will tell you anything that they think you want to hear. And I have to ask if it wasn't you, then who was it?"

"Lurch," answered Alice.

"Lurch? Who the fuck is Lurch?" exploded The Handler, before managing to keep his voice in check.

Alice raised a hand to pacify him. "Easy, easy. I don't know his name. He was a waiter at last night's event. He stood out because he was a little uncoordinated, so I gave him the name of Lurch. I saw him coming out of the exhibit."

"How convenient. My contact saw you coming out of the exhibit with your friend and the organiser. He didn't say anything about a mysteriously uncoordinated waiter. Besides, I vetted the staff list of the waiters, and they were all nobodies. Dancers, but not connected to anything else. So, do you know what I usually call people whose only alibi was that someone else did it and funnily enough, nobody else saw them do it?"

"What?" asked Alice, sure that she knew the answer and feeling herself become smaller on her seat.

"Dead."

The word hung in the air above them for a while. Alice had had enough and started to get up from her seat before The Handler made a *tssing* noise and she looked over and he had a pistol in his hand on his lap under the magazine. Her eyes widened and the gaping hole of the muzzle of the pistol filled her field of vision. She slumped back into her seat, not taking her eyes off the gun. She was vaguely aware of The Handler talking, but it was just background noise to her at this stage.

"Hey! I asked you a question," The Handler was saying. He hadn't raised his voice this time, but it was delivered in an insistent tone. "Who do you work for?"

"I work for SpareSpace—for Richard Grant. I write code for him."

The Handler watched her closely. "So, what are you doing here, then? Is he here? Are you here on an away day?" He smiled evilly. "I didn't think so."

Alice suddenly realised that he was going to kill her. Right here. In the foyer of this four-star airport hotel. As she made this realisation, far behind The Handler, she noticed Scott and Reggie leave the lift. The Handler's eyes did not leave hers and so she held his gaze, her mind racing with how she might tip the guys off to her predicament. She couldn't tip him off though, obviously. Before she could come up with a plan, they were gone from her view. All she got from her peripheral view was an image of Reggie looking down at two cell phones, one in each hand in confusion. *Great*, she thought, *he couldn't even figure out the guy in the room wasn't The Handler. So there won't be any squad breaking into the room.*

The Handler's eyes flicked behind Alice, presumably catching Scott and

Reggie leaving the hotel. He wasn't saying anything, but his eyes kept flicking between her eyes and whatever was going on behind her, either in the lounge or outside the hotel. While his attention was split he wasn't pulling the trigger, so Alice tried to come up with a plan where she could attract attention or otherwise make her escape.

"Get up," The Handler said, beckoning with his free hand. The other hand, holding the gun under the magazine was still trained on her. The magazine lay unnaturally draped over the gun, looking more like a Swiss chalet or an upside-down V. She got up and surveyed her surroundings. The reception area was vacant except for the employees behind the desk and as she rose Alice rotated until she could see what The Handler had been watching behind her. Reggie and Scott were nowhere to be seen—unsurprising really, as that was the plan. The Handler gestured towards the entrance and Alice started to walk in that direction. As she did so, The Handler moved alongside her with one arm around her waist. He smelled faintly of aftershave, and his shave was perfect. The other hand under the magazine was pointed at her midriff. They began walking towards the door when a group of four uniformed police officers, two of them holding submachine guns across their chests, came through the front doors. They didn't pause when they saw them but kept going into the lounge area beyond. The Handler tightened his left arm around Alice's midriff, but Alice didn't care because one of the police officers—no gun, but there in the second row had been Boris. He'd seen her immediately and had been about to speak but stopped himself as he saw her wide eyes staring meaningfully back. She didn't have to do anything more to communicate what was going on, she could see from the look on his eyes that he got it, he nodded and kept going inside. The Handler steered her along the corridor to the main doors of the hotel, the valet parkers loitering just outside plainly visible through the doors and the traffic along the A4 whizzing past beyond them.

Behind her, she heard a yell. "Armed Police! Drop the gun! We will shoot! Drop it!" She felt The Handler's grip on her tighten and he lifted her clear of the ground with his left arm, bodily carrying her as if she was something as inconsequential as a bag of shopping. She wasn't willing to go quietly though, and twisted her body causing her to slip from his grasp and fall to the ground. The armed police behind her wasted no time, barking commands and demanding The Handler alternately to drop his gun, get on the ground, move away from the girl and drop it, drop it! She wasn't really aware of what happened next because Boris was dragging her away from the scene back to the lounge area of the hotel foyer. She imagined at some point The Handler dropped the gun because there were no shots.

"Are you OK?" Boris asked.

"That fucking wanker," she complained, seething.

"It's ok, they've got him cuffed."

"Not him: Reggie. He fucked it all up and I was almost *killed*." The tension of the whole afternoon became too much and she dissolved into tears. Outside there was some sort of ruckus which resolved itself quickly and then there was silence. Alice slowly pulled herself together and looked up. Boris was returning from the cafe with a steaming cup of tea, the tag from the tea bag hanging on the outside of the recyclable cup. She sipped it as he revealed that he also had a bacon roll.

"Oh, I'm vegetarian, Boris," she said.

Boris looked confused. "Congratulations. Oh, this? No, this is for me, I haven't had anything to eat yet. Those SCO19 guys don't do breakfast."

Alice smiled. "What were you doing here?" she asked.

"Our friend Mike got me assigned to the team who were here for the takedown. As an unarmed extra, I hasten to add. Lucky for us that he did, otherwise they would have headed straight up to the hotel room, and we would have missed you."

"What was that noise before?"

"Before what?"

"After the arrest."

Boris grinned. "Oh, that? That was your friend Reggie. When they were taking The Handler to the car, all handcuffed, Reggie comes up and punches the guy square on the nose and yells 'Meredith says hello'. What the hell does that mean?"

Alice was feeling better now. "So what happens now?"

Boris patted her on the shoulder. "When you're feeling better, we'll head over to the station and take your statement for the record."

"I'm ready now, actually."

"Cool, let's go."

They headed back to the station, Boris taking her through the front desk to an interview room and recording her statement of what had happened as best she could recollect. She got a little choked up when she got to the part with the gun pointing at her and the arrest, but Boris put her at ease and she got through the process relatively painlessly.

"What happens now?"

"Well from a witness point of view, you're free to go."

"What happened to Scott?"

"Who's Scott?"

"He's the guy who took the sample—he was with Reggie when he called in the SWAT team."

"I think he might have gone home—why don't we go check?"

They moved from the interview room back into the situation room with the map on the wall. It had changed considerably since earlier that day and was a hive of activity. The armed police unit were just leaving, and Reggie was talking quietly on the phone while sitting on the floor in the corner with his back against the wall. Mike was talking to a uniformed officer and looked up when she walked in. He finished his conversation quickly and came over.

"Good work Boris, thanks for that. Alice, you were very brave, well done!"

Alice looked around the room. "Where is he?" she asked.

"The Handler? Oh, he's in the cells. Very secure, though he did need medical attention," Mike raised his voice, obviously pitching it for the benefit of Reggie, but he was engrossed in his own conversation.

Just then Mike's phone rang and he looked at the caller display. "Shit, sorry, I have to take this. Hello, sir. Yes, it was a good result, an excellent result. A good team effort, we pulled in a lot of favours.... I see.... Oh, I can understand that... That's not going to happen. No, this is not a pissing match, I'm not kicking up a fuss around jurisdiction. I'm going to secure my suspect and ensure that the police question him thoroughly. .... I'm sorry you feel that way, sir. Yes, I appreciate that. Thank you very much, I look forward to that." He looked up at Alice and Boris. "Well, things have already turned exciting." He noticed that Alice had been crying. "Are you alright? Have you had your statement taken yet?"

Alice nodded. "What was that all about?"

Mike shrugged. "Politics. It's illuminating who wants to take control of this particular prisoner before questioning starts. It's going to take a little while, but I'm hopeful that we get a lot of answers over the next few weeks."

"Thanks for inviting me onto the taskforce," said Boris.

"No problem, good work out there. We'll see if that goes some way to balancing the scales at your inquest," replied Mike.

"Which might not have been needed if Reggie hadn't gotten it wrong," Alice replied acerbically.

Mike frowned. "I think you might have that backwards, Alice. Reggie might have gotten the signals wrong, but that's what saved you. If we hadn't been called in, then we would have followed the decoy rather than coming in to take him down. The only reason we took down The Handler was because Boris saw you and reacted accordingly. He wouldn't have been there if we were holding back following the decoy. I think that's why The Handler thought it would be ok to approach you. He knew we'd be focusing on the decoy."

Alice still looked disgruntled.

"Look, head home. Get some rest. As soon as the papers find out what's happened, they're going to be swarming around the story and I'm not so sure you'll be able to slip under the radar like you did last time. Boris, thanks for your help, I'll make sure your new guvnor hears how you saved the day. Might pay to head back there now though."

Boris looked disappointed. "I was wondering if I could sit in on the questioning?"

Mike shook his head. "I'm afraid it's going to be a little busy in there—every man and his dog wants in on the questioning. I think everyone is expecting there to be some bombshells revealed."

"Aren't you afraid that something will happen to him in custody? Suicide? Or assisted non-consensual suicide?"

Mike nodded. "I've been running the phone hot, setting things up so that can't happen. Arranging isolated detention and round-the-clock supervision. It's harder than travel planning, I tell you." He winked. "We've got this, Alice. Go home. Get some rest. Thank you." He looked very sincerely at her. "Seriously, thank you for your help on this. We couldn't have gotten this guy without your help. Both of you. Now let me do my job," he said with a grin.

EPILOGUE

On a sunny weekend two weeks later, Alice was picked up from a train station in the middle of Sussex. The driver, a thickset man in his late fifties, didn't say much, just confirmed her identity before taking her wheelie bag and stashing it into the boot of the late model SUV. 'Eastwell Estate' was emblazoned in gold on the driver's door, a suitably official-looking coat of arms directly above the letters. The trip along the wooded country lanes didn't take long and, before she knew it, they had pulled off the road and were heading down a long driveway to a parking lot filled with half a dozen cars. The parking lot was in front of an impressive modern building three stories high. She could just make out an expanse of perfectly manicured lawn heading out to a lake beyond, and the house certainly seemed to be focused in that direction with a balcony on each of the first and second floors. Overlooking the parking lot were a smattering of windows and a ramp heading down into the bowels of the building. The driver extricated the suitcase, gruffly telling her that he'd take it to her room.

She followed him towards the front door where she was met by a short woman with silver hair fastened in a tight braid about the same age as the driver had been. and bustled out the front door to meet her.

"You must be Alice. I'm Meredith and I'm honoured to meet you. Mike has told us all about you and your adventures and we're really glad you decided to join us for the weekend. Before I forget, we've got you in a suite—top floor, room one—and here's your key. But I'll give you the tour first." She took Alice's arm and they walked around the front of the house. Meredith's accent was definitely from New Zealand, but softened, less pronounced. As the first glimpse had promised, there was a grand lawn leading up to a lake. Off to the left, a short path led to a kidney-shaped pool and a pool house which seemed at odds with the design of the rest of the mansion. She could now appreciate the size of the house—it was all glass and chrome, huge floor-to-ceiling windows and glass-edged balconies. Meredith kept up a running commentary as they went.

"We redeveloped about a year after the Insurrection was put down, but it took two years for the insurance situation to be resolved. With so many claims, a lot of the insurance companies went under, you see. The government had to step in. Well, they didn't *have* to, but the people making the claims were all the lords and posh folk, so the government was under a lot of pressure. So they underwrote half of the claims. Which meant that most people only got a pay out of half of what their property was worth. A bit sad. Some folk couldn't afford to rebuild, and a lot of people sold up."

Alice frowned. "So you were able to rebuild before the insurance money came through?"

Meredith smiled. "Well, Reggie had a stroke of luck. One of his books was going to be made into a film in the US before the Insurrection happened. So those relationships were in place with perfect timing for the screenplay he wrote about the events. One thing led to another and before you know it, that movie 'The Bunker' was greenlit and made and doing well. The option on that, plus the option on the already-in-production movie allowed us to get a head-start on the building, and we were able to borrow against the government pay out, so we were ahead of the curve."

"Wait, was that here? The movie, I mean."

"Yes, back when 'here' was a mock Tudor mansion."

"So was Ingenue staying here when it happened?"

"Yes, she's floating around here somewhere. I'll make sure you meet her, if you like?"

"That would be cool, thanks for that."

A line of tents had been set up down one side of the lawn, multi-coloured bunting strung up between them and the smell of cooking and the sizzle of a barbeque wafting over from there. A few figures lurked near where the smells and sounds were coming from and one of them raised a pair of tongs in greeting before turning back to the plumpish woman beside him. Obviously, a cooking discussion.

"You've met Reggie, of course?" Meredith continued. She noticed Alice's change in demeanour at the mention of his name. They continued their walk, arm in arm towards the house, a patio out the front leading inside through giant French doors into an open-plan lounge/kitchen. "He feels incredibly badly with how the hotel operation went. I guess it was a bit much to expect him to recognise someone he'd seen for maybe two minutes, three years ago."

Alice gently removed her arm from Meredith's and looked at her intently. "I could have been killed!"

Meredith nodded. "That's true. That's what he's been torturing himself with since then. I keep telling him what happened was a lucky accident, because it led to you being saved, but he doesn't see it that way. And I see that you don't either. But I heard he punched Sebastian. Is that true?"

Alice smirked. And then nodded. "He said that you said hello right before hitting him, apparently."

Meredith smiled broadly, before turning back to the house. "We wanted a more open living and dining area but didn't want the cooking to be something which happens in secret. So, what had been four different rooms in the original design turned into this one large room."

A couple was talking on comfortable couches in the corner of the lounge, but they looked up when Alice and Meredith got nearer. The man was short with a runner's lean and wiry build, hardly an ounce of fat on him. He got up as they approached to introduce himself. "Hi, I'm Gavin," he said, extending a hand. Alice shook it politely, trying not to stare at the woman he'd been talking to. Ingenue also stood and shook her hand.

"I'm Ingenue," she stated with a smile. Even in casual clothes, she exuded elegance.

"This is Alice, she's the one who apprehended Sebastian Miller two weeks ago."

The other two beamed appreciatively as Alice protested that the police were the ones who had done the arresting. Ingenue sat back down and patted the couch beside her. Gavin smiled welcomingly and Meredith asked if Alice would like a drink. She noticed that both Gavin and Ingenue had long glasses with mint leaves mingling with ice cubes at the surface. "Maybe one of those?" she replied.

"One mojito, coming up!" said Meredith, heading towards the kitchen.

"Now, tell me *everything*," said Ingenue.

Gavin burst into laughter. "Careful, she's angling for her next role—I'd insist on a cut if I was you!"

Alice spent an enjoyable half hour talking with the pair of them, their drinks being refreshed periodically by Meredith or one of the waitstaff doing the rounds. It was fascinating talking to Ingenue about the differences between the movie and the reality of her experiences in the original mansion. Gavin turned out to be some sort of whiz with satellites and had been visiting the country for a conference where he was presenting. For her part, the story of her undercover adventures was met with a slightly glazed look (when she was talking about the coding and cryptography) and squeals of excitement (from both Gavin and Ingenue) when she related the sting operation and tracking down the remote-control cars.

"Seriously, though, has anyone talked to you about making a movie about your story?" Ingenue asked.

Alice blinked in surprise. "I hadn't thought about that," she replied. "The papers got my number somehow and it's been ringing off the hook with offers for telling them my story, but I've kind of been in recovery mode."

Ingenue leaned in as if she was about to let Alice into her confidence. "I'll let you into a little secret—my book was ghost-written! If I can get a book written in six months and a movie made in a year, think what you could do."

"I'll definitely give that some thought," said Alice. "Ooh—someone has just come in that I want to catch up with—talk later?"

Ingenue and Gavin resumed their conversation as Alice got up and walked over to talk to Boris. After mutual agreement that it was indeed great to see each other, they walked over to the kitchen to get Boris a beer and then found a seat out on the patio overlooking the tents on the lawn.

They watched as a crate of bottles was brought out by the driver of the SUV and set up in one of the tents, and Reggie flitted between the bottles and the barbeque area. Boris was watching her watch Reggie.

"You don't like him do you?"

"You weren't the one with a gun pointed at you."

Boris nodded. "That's true, but that's not his fault, is it? By all accounts, you were in the foyer instead of being in the safety of the situation room, or your own home, or *anywhere* else because you wanted Scott to be comfortable taking the samples. Is it Reggie that you are really angry at?" He took a long swallow of beer before giving her another of his searching looks.

Alice wanted very much to change the subject. "So one thing I didn't tell you was a weird thing that The Handler—sorry, Sebastian—said to me in the foyer, while he was holding the gun on me."

Boris frowned, puzzled. "Ok..."

"He thought that I had stolen a million pounds from him." She told him of the heist and about Lurch.

"Sounds interesting, but it would be very difficult to get anyone to sanction an investigation into a theft against public enemy number one."

"That's what I thought. The perfect crime, if you can get away with it, right? A million pounds." She got a faraway look in her eyes, thinking about what she could do with a million pounds. Boris waited a bit and then broke her reverie.

"Oh, good news, the investigation found that although I had done unspeakable things and had a permanent blot on my record, there were enough mitigating circumstances and good work—arresting Sebastian—

that meant that something normally considered gross misconduct would be treated—in this case only—as merely misconduct and therefore warranted a written warning rather than dismissal."

"Hey, that's great! Awesome! Oh, speak of the devil," Alice said, pointing with her chin towards the path leading up to the house. Mike was walking towards them, holding a gift-wrapped bottle of wine in his hands.

Boris and Mike shook hands and Mike kissed her on the cheek before excusing himself, saying that he had to say hello to their hosts. He returned five minutes later, having swapped the gift-wrapped bottle of wine for a bottle of beer. He settled into one of the patio chairs and sighed.

"So, how goes the questioning?" asked Boris.

Mike took a swig of his beer and relaxed into his chair. "Much better than a week ago. We've certainly made a breakthrough. Strange goings-on though."

"Oh?" asked Alice, leaning forward.

"Yes, you know that there was a certain level of political interference when we first made the arrest? The Foreign Office wanted to be involved."

Boris frowned. "But the arrest was made in the UK. Of a UK citizen."

"I know, right? The argument there was that it could potentially have an adverse effect on our international relations. That was easy enough to kill, but it did give me an insight into some of the people who may not want us to speak to our friend Sebastian, who at that stage was keeping very quiet. Fair enough, that's his right, right? Anyway, we expected him to be represented by his top-notch lawyers—the ones that your friend Richard Grant over at SpareSpace employs. But they didn't show up and I was a little curious, so I reached out and apparently our man Sebastian hadn't paid his bill. And in that first week, despite various overtures to other top-notch lawyers, there was a distinct lack of interest in the case. I'm not sure whether that was because of the outstanding fees side of things, or the fact that he was public enemy number one. Either way, he's been much more interested in conversing with us this week. He had a rather optimistic view of his bargaining position that I had to explain to him was rooted more in fantasy than in reality. I mentioned that there were some newspapers that wanted to get the CPS to charge him with one count of murder for every person who died in the Insurrection. Even if he managed to get those knocked down to a manslaughter charge, if he served them concurrently he would be behind bars for a few centuries. He thought he'd be able to share the names of those on the inside that helped or turned a blind eye and he'd get out scot-free, but now he knows the most he could get for that information is a more comfortable cell. And so he's becoming a little more 'sharing', shall we say."

Alice was impressed. "So you've got your guy, you're going to get the insiders who allowed the Insurrection to happen—happy ending all around, right?"

Boris shook his head with a wry smile. "I imagine that anyone who is exposed by Sebastian may end up having multiple layers of protection. It's going to take a lot of political nous to get them all, right Mike?"

Mike nodded. "But that's a challenge for another day. In the meantime, there's hot food to eat, cold drinks to drink and good company to share them both with. I'm hoping to get a tour of the bunkers at some point—unless they removed them when they remodelled?"

Alice shrugged. "I'm sure Ingenue will know, let's go and ask her." They collected their drinks and trooped inside to where Ingenue and Gavin were still deep in conversation. As she followed the others inside, Alice looked over her shoulder at Reggie, still organising the barbeque and Meredith bustling beside him. Maybe she *had* been too hard on him.

Mike went over to Gavin and greeted him very warmly—Alice wasn't sure quite how Gavin fitted into the party, but from the looks of it Mike was involved. Ingenue got up and started to lead the way out of the room, trailed by Boris. Gavin and Mike followed next and Alice brought up the rear, which was the perfect spot to eavesdrop on Mike and Gavin's conversation.

"So how did the satellite fit in? I followed the news about the insurrection, but couldn't see how that was relevant."

"It turns out that the people behind the insurrection were moving a shipment of arms into the country. The distribution sites would have been quite obvious to any surveillance based in space, and so that camouflaged satellite was invaluable for keeping them hidden. Plus, the people involved were doing drills and training in the countryside, which would have been very easy to spot from the air."

"But why did the Russians allow their satellite to be used like that? That must have been a diplomatic nightmare after they were found out?"

Mike made the universal sign for money, rubbing the tops of his fingers against the top of his thumb. "They didn't think that they would get caught— especially when they tried it out over New Zealand. We got lucky with your data. And they got paid by The Handler. He made a lot of money out of the whole insurrection. That's why we were so keen on catching him."

"And if he was paying the Russians for using their satellite, who was giving money to him?"

By this time, they had made their way to one of the other rooms in the house on the ground floor, a large rug on the floor pulled to one side and a door open and leading down into the dark. Ingenue let out a squeal of delight at the tall figure leaving the stairs on his way up. A bespectacled young man looked up in surprise and they embraced, filling the room with excited chatter as Boris looked on in bemused silence. Alice was caught between continuing her eavesdropping of Mike and Gavin's conversation and the louder and more effusive declarations between Ingenue and the newcomer.

Apparently, the new guy was someone named Marcus and he was in trouble for not getting in touch with Ingenue to let her know that he was in the country. Marcus on the other hand would be starting a semester in Oxford as part of his degree and was spending some time back with his uncle before school started. Ingenue noticed Mike glance around to see if anyone was listening before stepping off to one side with Gavin and continuing their conversation. Alice was still close enough to just make out what was said.

"It was actually a group of well-connected lords and ladies who had a grudge against another group of similarly aristocratic people. They encouraged and provoked a fringe political group and then arranged with The Handler to arm them. They influenced their hit lists to make sure their competitors were first for the chop and made sure that they were safe when everything kicked off. It wasn't perfect—there were a few mansions and estates lost when the insurgents went off-piste, but they pretty much got what they were after. Except, their goal was to lance the boil of the common people—their words, not mine—and then consolidate their power even further after the false flag uprising. But it looks like the sympathies of the people are swinging the other way—the current polls are showing more support for the working classes. And The Handler has flipped on his employers, meaning that we will be paying some quiet visits to a few of the good and the great and of course their legal teams and explain to them that we have a rather good case against them."

Gavin frowned as he took it all in. "And will they be convicted?"

Mike shrugged as he smiled at the rambunctious reunion on the other side of the room. "Well, I'll be trying my best to get as many of them as possible. We'll see how successful I am. We're going against some of the oldest families in the country. They've got a lot of friends in high places." He smiled at Gavin. "But I've got friends of my own." He turned back to the door set into the floor. "Now, let's check out this bunker, shall we?"

Alice couldn't restrain herself. "I'm sorry, Mike, I couldn't help overhearing your conversation. Are you seriously telling me that all of that *stuff* was a fight between a bunch of toffs?"

Mike looked around to see if anyone else was listening. Ingenue and Marcus had headed down the stairs into the bunker, followed by Boris, so it was just Alice, Mike and Gavin.

"Well, it didn't start like that, no," he said at last. "Apparently there was some government contract which two competing syndicates were contesting. Each had their friends within the government lobbying the decision-makers to hand the juicy contract to their friends. Once they realised that the other group existed, the lobbying deteriorated into dirty tricks and smear campaigns. One of which was trying to connect the opposition to the '99%'. Connecting your competitors to a loud and embarrassing but fundamentally powerless political movement wasn't damning enough, so they provided a few nudges, a bit of funding and cover from scrutiny by the intelligence forces. And one thing leads to another and you find yourself with the worst armed insurrection ever undertaken, a few thousand lives lost, and a pretty significant shuffle of the upper classes. Maybe even electoral reform. The most interesting part is that out of a run-of-the-mill greedy cash-grab has come some of the most meaningful debate and discussion of the class system this nation has ever seen."

"That's crazy!"

"I would caution you both that what you've heard is not common knowledge and you would be in breach of the Official Secrets Act if you said anything to anyone else about it."

"Sure... sure..." said Alice, looking back out across the open lawn festooned with tents and streamers. It certainly was a weird and wonderful world they all lived in.

ABOUT THE AUTHOR

C.G. Lambert was born the second of seven children and raised in South Auckland, New Zealand. His pre-writing career consisted of applying for whatever job sounded interesting, leading to time as an International Banker, a Music Manager, Web Developer and Analytics Manager. He loves travel (you can read about it at etrip.tips), holds dual citizenship (NZ/UK), a Bachelor of Arts and an MBA. He currently resides in the UNESCO City of Literature—Edinburgh—with his long term partner.

You can find out more at cglambert.com

HOW IT ALL BEGAN
C.G. LAMBERT
Book One
in the
Uncle Reggie
Stories
THE
KIDS WHO
LIVED IN A
HOLE

WHAT HAPPENED TO UNCLE REGGIE?

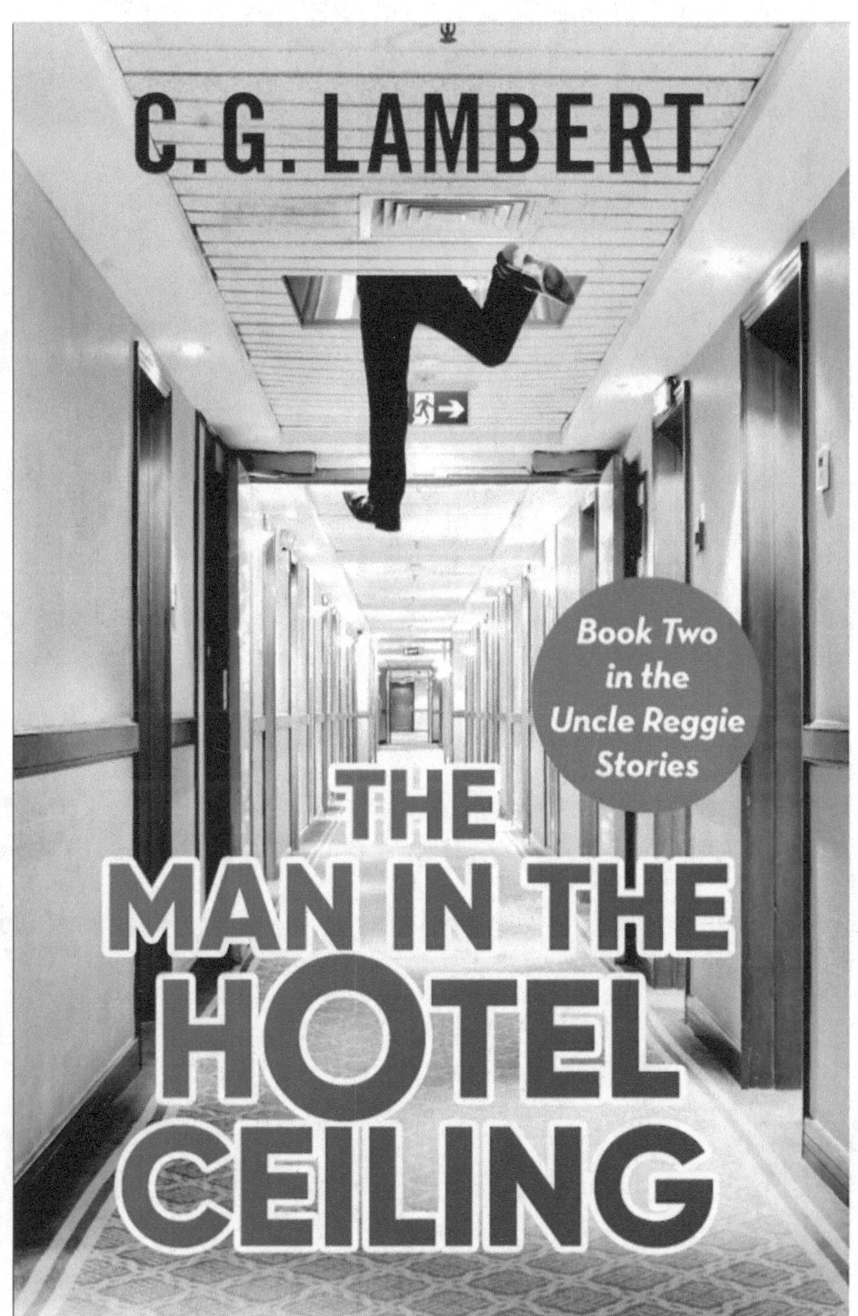
C. G. LAMBERT
Book Two
in the
Uncle Reggie
Stories
THE
MAN IN THE
HOTEL
CEILING